Hell To Pay

The Life and Violent Times of Eli Gault

J. LEE BUTTS

BERKLEY BOOKS, NEW YORK

THE BERKLEY PUBLISHING GROUP
Published by the Penguin Group
Penguin Group (USA) Inc.
375 Hudson Street, New York, New York 10014, USA
Penguin Group (Canada), 90 Eglinton Avenue East, Suite 700, Toronto, Ontario M4P 2Y3, Canada
(a division of Pearson Penguin Canada Inc.)
Penguin Books Ltd., 80 Strand, London WC2R 0RL, England
Penguin Group Ireland, 25 St. Stephen's Green, Dublin 2, Ireland (a division of Penguin Books Ltd.)
Penguin Group (Australia), 250 Camberwell Road, Camberwell, Victoria 3124, Australia
(a division of Pearson Australia Group Pty. Ltd.)
Penguin Books India Pvt. Ltd., 11 Community Centre, Panchsheel Park, New Delhi—110 017, India
Penguin Group (NZ), 67 Apollo Drive, Rosedale, North Shore 0632, New Zealand
(a division of Pearson New Zealand Ltd.)
Penguin Books (South Africa) (Pty.) Ltd., 24 Sturdee Avenue, Rosebank, Johannesburg 2196,
South Africa

Penguin Books Ltd., Registered Offices: 80 Strand, London WC2R 0RL, England

This is a work of fiction. Names, characters, places, and incidents either are the product of the author's imagination or are used fictitiously, and any resemblance to actual persons, living or dead, business establishments, events, or locales is entirely coincidental. The publisher does not have any control over and does not assume any responsibility for author or third-party websites or their content.

HELL TO PAY

A Berkley Book / published by arrangement with the author

PRINTING HISTORY
Berkley edition / July 2009

Copyright © 2009 by J. Lee Butts.
Cover illustration by Bill Angresano.
Interior text design by Laura K.Corless.

ISBN: 978-0-425-22865-4

BERKLEY®
Berkley Books are published by The Berkley Publishing Group,
a division of Penguin Group (USA) Inc.,
375 Hudson Street, New York, New York 10014.
BERKLEY® is a registered trademark of Penguin Group (USA) Inc.
The "B" design is a trademark of Penguin Group (USA) Inc.

PRINTED IN THE UNITED STATES OF AMERICA

10   9   8   7   6   5   4   3   2   1

1

Uvalde, Texas, 1882

"Yes, brothers and sisters, there is a Hell."

Way I've got it figured, most decent, respectable people will likely give little credence to the story of how I now find myself in such a sorry state. Little doubt about it, there's gonna be hell to pay for my manifest and bloody sins. Truth be told, I blame my father, the Reverend Joshua Gault—a fire-breathing evangelist who traveled the Texas countryside in a ramshackle covered wagon preaching the Gospel—for the entire ugly mess that has been my life.

Pa's torturous path to false righteousness proved an impossible one for an irredeemable sinner such as me. Upon his head I lay all the blood I've spilled, all the grief I've caused, all my murders. You can find my butchery buried in the subtext of his sermons, in the nightly beatings he administered upon my person, and carved on a wicked heart hidden behind the collar of a man of the cloth—a man possessed by the spirit of a most vengeful God.

My mother gave up the twisted journey down Pa's long

and narrow road to salvation two years after presenting me to an unsuspecting world—in the Year of Our Lord 1862. As the only child of their fractious and destructive union, I endured a virtual hell on earth during the fifteen years that followed that poor woman's tragic passing.

Little doubt has ever existed in my mind, or heart, that the evil old bastard blamed me for my mother's unfortunate demise. According to the Reverend, hers was the first blood I spilled. Mighty hard for a child to bear the burden of such an accusation. If I showed signs of forgetting his feelings on the subject, thrashings that ofttimes brought me near death served as the falsely sanctified redeemer's gentle reminders of his view on the matter.

I hereby publicly confess to all my past sins and beg the Lord's forgiveness, but swear upon the altar of the real Jehovah that the killing I now face final judgment for is one I did not commit. At worst, my part in the man's death was no more than a simple case of self-defense.

My earliest, and most dreadful, memories always return to my father. I grew nigh to manhood being forced to sit on the "amen" pew while he delivered his hellfire-and-brimstone sermons to crowds of the ignorant but faithful. Those poor dirt-digging goobers gathered in flimsy church buildings, in cornfields, on dirt roads and byways all over the Great Lone Star State just to hear the crazed son of a bitch rant and rave. Have to give him his due, though. Pa was good at the soul saving trade and possessed an uncommon skill as an orator and consummate actor.

We dragged an ancient piece of oak podium he'd stolen from an office building in Dallas—on my thirteenth birthday no less—all over hell and gone so he'd have something to hang on to during his sermons. He'd get all worked up and grab the top of that battered chunk of wood like an exhausted swimmer in the arms of a drowning lover headed for the bottom. You couldn't have pried his claw-like fingers loose with a crowbar. Rivers of sweat streamed down a dreadful face, twisted with rage and false concern. His stern gaze would sweep over all those anxious for the Lord's saving blessings, like waves during ole Noah's little rainstorm.

Sometimes, he fingered at pages in The Book, or perhaps read a fearsome passage from Revelations. Then the crazy bastard would launch into an act I must have seen a thousand times over the years. Ole Josh would start off slow, like a winded racehorse, and build the tease to a feverish, screeching pitch.

"Yes, brothers and sisters, there is a Hell." That particular piece of information seemed of unending interest to those lacking anything in the way of worldly sophistication.

"Amen, Brother Gault." The sweat-stained and dirty-finger nailed shouted their faith in fervent response.

"Those not saved by the blood will certainly see that horrid place 'where the worm never dies, but the fire is quenched not.' Where Satan awaits your arrival and revels in the prospect of hearing your eternal screams for mercy."

"Amen. Lead us home, sweet Jesus."

"Save us, Reverend Gault." The reaction from his overheated audience bordered on thunderous.

A subtle urgency usually crept into his voice at this point. "Oh, ye dam-ned sinners, the day will come when you stand in judgment before the Golden Book of the Lamb."

"Take us, Lord."

"Bless us, Jesus."

"Lord God above." The reaction was louder than before.

"An angel's sacred finger will trace the gilded lines till he finds your name. His beatific smile will vanish as he asks a single question, brothers and sisters, 'Are you saved?'"

"Oh sweet, merciful Father."

"Deliver us, Jesus."

"Lead on, Brother Gault. Lead on." His entire faithful congregation now bordered on hysteria.

He'd oblige by aggressively shaking an accusatory finger in each and every face. Then he'd screech, "And you'll be forced to answer that saintly Being with a resounding, 'No. I am not.' At that very moment, dear sinner, you'll realize your immortal soul is doomed, damned to the squirming, fiery pit for time without end."

"Merciful heavens," shrieked his terrified audiences.

"Deliver us from the fiery pit, Reverend."

Pa knew he had them in the palm of his hand, so he'd really start bearing down on the poor bastards. "You have to save yourselves." Up went the Bible, and he whacked the podium with it. Hard-fisted rap sounded like a pistol shot. Womenfolk in the choir and front row sometimes fainted.

"If you truly believe, stand up. Come down the aisle. Humbly kneel before God's chosen messenger and publicly demonstrate to this gathering the sincerity of your faith."

Whack went his Bible against the podium top. Second time sounded like thunder on Judgment Day. His bony, shuddering finger waved in their horrified faces.

"Confess your sins before Almighty God and this company. No matter how rancid and disgusting you may think your immortal soul has become during a lifetime of transgressions against the Word, there's still time to avoid the fires of perdition."

My God, people panicked by the prospect of damnation fought each other to make it down the aisle first. "Lead me back to the flock, Preacher. I've lied. I've cheated, stole from my friends, and consumed alcoholic spirits."

"Oh, sweet merciful God, I've *fornicated* with my neighbor's wife," some squealed.

That last one usually started a fistfight after the services. Have to admit, I used to love to hear them fornicators confess. Knew we'd see a little extra in the way of entertainment that night. Almost had a killing one evening when a pissed-off husband went at one of the fornicators with an ax. But the poor angry cuckold only managed to separate the malefactor from a few of his fingers and toes. Scene was still mighty bloody, decorated with body parts, and loads of fun to watch.

If the response from the congregation didn't match Pa's covetous and fevered expectations, he'd go damn near frantic. See, he realized the amount in the offering plates was heavily influenced by the number of folks heading up the aisle for his version of salvation. Evil skunk had to save a bunch of souls if he wanted to make any money.

"Once you've admitted before God's appointed angel that you've never been washed in the blood of the Lamb, it's too late. The yawning pit of everlasting damnation will open before your very feet." Pa was preaching so fast, sometimes I couldn't even follow him.

He'd let that last part sit on them poor sinners' hearts for a second or so, and then launch off again. "Sulfurous steam rising from the burning bodies of Hell's most wretched will befoul your nostrils. The greasy, filth-covered tentacles of Satan's imps will slither up your quaking legs. Gather your shrieking soul into the Fiend's front parlor. You pitiable wretches can look forward to being nothing more than sport for impish torture—forevermore. Is that what you want, brethren?" At that point, he had reached a screech level that usually caused me to cover my ears. Always wondered how the man's throat could stand such punishment.

God in Heaven, sometimes the stampede got damn near unbelievable. Once, in a little pissant town called Ballentyne, an old man almost got stomped to death when he fell about halfway down the aisle. Concerned members of the congregation took near ten minutes to untangle the mass of people on top of the poor old goat.

Yes indeed, the Reverend Joshua Gault, loved and admired by earnest Christian folk all over Texas, laughed like hell for years after he finished his sermon the night that old man fell on his face. He'd suck up a quart of Old Overcoat, beat on the little table in our covered wagon, hoot like a strangled owl, and into the darkness of black night yelp, "Oh, my glorious God, took everything I could do to keep from laughing. Poor son of a bitch went down in the aisle like a felled tree. Had hobnailed heel marks all over his wrinkled old ass when we finally retrieved him."

When all else failed to generate the response he fully expected, Pa would get so serious, you'd of thought God was coming after everyone in the whole damned world that very minute. He'd scream, "Ye damnable sinners, you can either love Jesus and confess it to the world, or go to Hell and forever burn. Which is it going to be? Do you want eternal life or a festering, pustulated, scab-covered damnation?" If that one didn't work, for damned sure, nothing would.

Sometimes, we'd pass that plate three or four times before he got the right amount—in other words, enough for a bottle of whiskey and a night with any fallen woman who happened to be handy. If there weren't any fallen ones available, he'd often help himself to one of the lonely, more-than-willing, thunderstruck widow ladies attending his service.

Seemed to me as though whiskey and a willing woman was all he required to stay alive. Hell, I needed food and damn near starved to death at times. 'Course life with the Reverend wasn't all bad. I did get a damned fine education. My worthless father knew more about the Bible than any man I ever met, and he could quote Shakespeare like one of them stage actor fellers. Had me reading The Book and the tragedies before I'd turned ten years old.

I'll never forget the fateful night of our parting. Happened a few weeks after my seventeenth birthday. I was a big strapping kid by then. Looked like a fully growed man. Over six feet tall, like Pa, stringy-muscled and hard as a rock. Remember the event like it was yesterday.

We made a stop in the tiny village of La Honda. A full moon, pale as wicked death, big as a dinner plate, and shrouded in silver clouds, hung in a pitch-black sky. Pa had sucked up more than a few snorts of the devil's brew. I could tell early on the evening wouldn't end well for me. Never did when he went on one of his whiskey-swilling binges. Always dreaded seeing him come home with a jug in his hand.

He was one of those drunks who would be the finest feller you ever met one minute and a raving, vengeful loon the next. As he'd done hundreds of times before, the man went totally wild—his last night amongst the living.

We'd suffered through a particularly poor collection that evening. Just didn't matter one damned bit. Pa still managed to scratch up enough money for a bottle of locally brewed corn liquor. Hit that jug pretty hard. Must have consumed damned near all of it in less than an hour. He got drunker than Cooter Brown. Lit into me with his belt a damn sight earlier than usual. Thought he'd beat me slap to death. That whipping was the worst he ever put on me.

About the tenth time his brass buckle bounced off my spine, something inside my brain snapped like a rotten cottonwood branch. Grabbed up a shovel we sometimes used to dig our wagon out of the mud on those rare occasions when it managed to rain in South Texas. Busted him across the face with it. Blood splattered from one side of the wagon to the other. He kind of grunted, and then dropped like a piece of beefsteak on a red-hot skillet. Guess I must have cut an artery or something equally as important to staying alive. Blood spewed from his neck like water from one of them hand-pump fire wagons.

For the first time in my life, I knew exactly what the word "bloodlust" meant. Went at him like one of them demons he preached on so often. Beat on the man till my arms ached like I'd been digging graves. Finished up when the shovel handle broke, and realized I was almost ankle deep in blood and gore. Nasty business.

Carried the shovel into the woods. Dug a hole. Pushed the dirt in over the murder weapon and my saturated clothing with my bare, bloody hands. Covered the newly turned earth with all the leaves I could find. Scratched over everything with a tree limb to make it as natural- and undisturbed-looking as possible. Bathed all his blood away in a nearby creek. Walked back to the wagon nekkid as the day my mother birthed me. Put on clean clothes and headed for the La Honda town marshal's office.

Beat on that lawman's door and hollered like a wounded animal. Cried buckets of tears when I told as how I'd come back from fishing in the creek and found my poor beloved father beat to death by some foul, murdering skunk who'd stolen every penny we'd saved over the last ten years. 'Course there weren't no family fortune. Evil, Bible-thumping son of a bitch drank up ever penny we ever made. But that tiny falsehood made my tale sound better.

Lying, trickery, and a talent for acting came my way naturally. I was good at it, just like my old man. Silly marshal, and everyone else in town, ate it up like bread pudding with apples and raisins.

Dim-witted local lawman's investigation found the murder exactly the way I'd described it. Them poor La Honda boobs never suspected me for a second. Mysteriously, anonymous killers have always held a certain appeal to the ignorant and ill-informed. Hell, them melon-headed tater-diggers even put out a wanted poster for any information leading to the arrest of the "unknown" murderous thieves who took the life of poor, and much beloved, Reverend Joshua Gault. Amen, brothers and sisters. Pass the plate.

2

"Eli done went and stabbed Harvey."

La Honda Ladies' Aid Society drew me under its sheltering wing. They even took up a *love offering* of almost two hundred dollars to offset the loss of my stolen family fortune. More money than my pa had ever managed to collect at any of his revivals. Dear, sweet, sainted ladies even arranged for me to live with a family name of Hickerson that had migrated from the smoky hills of Tennessee. Stayed with them folks for two years.

Leader of that group of concerned women, a Mrs. Crumpton, cried and prayed over me for months. Wept as she told Mrs. Hickerson, "The poor babe is left in a heartless world. Alone. Abandoned to the vagaries of cruel fate. Foully murdered father. No mother. Why, it's just a tragic situation, Estel. Can't you see your way to taking him in? Our organization is willing to help with all expenses involving his education. We'll even pay twenty dollars a month toward his room and board."

On the surface of it, those Hickersons seemed like nice people, but the whole clan had something of a mean-assed greedy streak in them, too. They let me move into a tiny room not much bigger than a closet. Entire family met me on the porch and made quite a show of taking me in.

Hickersons had a daughter—the lovely Charlotte. I didn't know much about girls. Had tried my hand with a few along the trail. But I was young and had lots to learn. My pa had always kept me under a sanctimoniously heavy thumb whole time he was breathing. Wicked wretch often preached sermons especially for my ears in the back of our wagon. Always ranted about original sin, the horrifically destructive path women could lead a man down, and how their carnal company virtually insured a good man's place in a blistering Hell. And if that didn't do the job, he'd describe, in horrifying detail, the numerous life-threatening diseases carried by any willing female. Set me to wondering why he spent so much time with 'em.

Hadn't been in the Hickerson house but one day when Charlotte passed me in the hall. Gal grabbed me by the crotch and squeezed the hell out of it. I tried to grab hers, but she scampered away. God Almighty, from then on I wanted to put my hands in Charlotte's drawers so bad, I almost exploded every time that gal got near me. Lust-possessed she-devil knew it, too. Female spawn from Hell's deepest circle used to tease me something unmerciful.

She'd catch me sitting at the table reading the sacred word of God, then lean down and stick her tongue in my ear. One time, whilst I was taking my weekly bath, she tiptoed into my room and before I knew what was happening, that gal had grabbed what she'd been after since the day I arrived. Held on like a Louisiana snapping turtle—'cept it felt real good. Then she must've heard something, 'cause she left me stewing in my own juices. I almost passed out.

Charlotte's room was right next to mine. Had a nice-sized hole in the wall I could look through and watch her undress. Pretty certain she knew about that peephole. Hell, she might have even carved out that opening her very own self, for all I know. Wouldn't put it past her— given how iniquitous Pa said gals and women could be.

Randy gal spent most of her conscious moments tempting me to give up my immortal soul and run with horned Satan. She made my blood run cold and hot— along with lots of other more indecent things that went on in my own drawers.

Always got the feeling she enjoyed shedding her clothes for an appreciative audience. And that ain't all, by a long damned shot. Gal would fondle herself. Goddamn, her sinful behavior like to have drove me buggier than a horse blanket full of brown dog ticks. Made my relationship with God mighty difficult, and seemed to be pulling me closer to the Devil's work each and every time I took a peep at her nekkid flesh.

Guess I'd been living with them for two months or so when Mr. Hickerson put me to cleaning out the hayloft of his barn. Charlotte snuck up from behind, grabbed me around my waist, and jammed her hand into my pants. Stuck her tongue in my ear and licked me till I almost passed out.

Then she whispered, "You are one good-looking boy, Eli. All them sweaty muscles. And, God almighty, you're as hard as the head on a miner's pick. Makes me wet just looking at you. Bet you'd like to stick that sweet pecker of yours inside me, wouldn't you?"

Gal scared the righteous hell out of me. I twirled around, dropped the pitchfork, and almost stepped on the thing barefoot. She had the front of her dress tucked up in her belt. Damned if you couldn't see everything Charlotte had, and that gal had plenty. She was staring wide-eyed at the bulge in the crotch of my coveralls. Seemed mesmerized like one of them chickens what gets charmed by a snake.

My father's thunderous voice rumbled up from his

shallow grave and cut through my brain like a hay sickle. Think that put a fear in me worse than Charlotte's brazen nekkidness. His bloody ghost bellowed, "You'll burn, boy. Satan is about to drag your dumb ass to the fiery pit. Betwixt that gal's luscious legs lies the juicy highway to a smoldering Hell. Beelzebub's gonna take uncommon joy when he roasts that evil appendage of your over his everlasting inferno. Run away, boy, run away. The bonfires of Hell are licking at your heels." Think he might have meant some other area of my body, or maybe I just heard him wrong.

Then, damnation, Charlotte started making these nasty hunching motions at me. Grabbed herself betwixt the legs, fell over backward into the hay, and went to moaning like she was dying. Shit, that scared me even worse. Thought I might have done something by accident—maybe poked her with the pitchfork and killed her.

Boy, I was about as far off the mark as a poor ignorant-assed wretch could be. She sat up, motioned for me to come to her, and said, "Do it to me, Eli. I really need it."

Now, I want it known here that I tried to heed The Book's teachings. Said a hasty, but silent, prayer and looked to Heaven for guidance. Couldn't see a damned thing but Mr. Hickerson's barn rafters. The Lord must have been busy with something more important in another county. But, hell, I waited and hoped maybe an angel would show up. If God sent one, it took him way too long to find the barn. Must of got lost up in Austin.

After about a minute's worth of serious praying, I just couldn't hold back any longer. Don't know what got into me. Thought my head was gonna explode—amongst other things. Went totally bat-shit moonstruck nuts. Jumped on Charlotte's beautifully shaped nekkid ass like a rutting pig.

We must have fornicated on every flat surface in ole man Hickerson's hayloft. Twice. Maybe three times. Think I might have gone completely crazy during the act. Felt like my entire body flew to pieces at one point.

Strangest of all, the hair on my entire head vibrated like picked banjo strings for almost an hour. And from then on, till I had to leave town, Charlotte couldn't keep her hands off me. Girl was like an East Texas forest fire—unquenchable.

At first, I really enjoyed doing the dirty deed, you know. So much to see and touch, and all that new stuff to learn. But, hell, after a while, the whole act got to be something akin to work. Charlotte was clawing at the front of my pants every time I turned around. Never cared much for school before, but I was actually glad when class took up that fall. She was a year older, attended the group ahead of mine, and had to leave me alone—at least during the daytime anyway.

Like I said before, she was one fine-looking gal. Naturally, the other boys spent most of their waking moments sniffing around like a pack of dogs chasing a bitch in heat any chance they got. And, truth be told, she probably let some of them hump her, too. I didn't care all that much. So long as they didn't make a big deal out of doing the horizontal wiggle with her.

But about halfway through the school term of my last year, she must have let Harvey Bryant get a little of that stuff on his pecker. Mouthy son of a bitch went and bragged to every other man and boy in three counties about it. Made me madder than I'd ever been in my entire life. Not even the night I killed Pa fired me up like Harvey's filthy bragging.

Caught him behind the schoolhouse one day and said, "Harvey, you'd best keep your mouth shut when it comes to Charlotte. I hear any more nasty stories about her that I can trace back to you, and I'll kick your bony ass till your nose bleeds."

Dumb son of a bitch laughed right in my face. Sneered at me like I was something green and gooey he'd found stuck to the bottom of his boot. Said, "Well, you can kiss my bony ass, Gault. You don't tell nobody named Bryant how to act or what to say. Bet you're humpin' her yourself. Damn near every man in McLennan County's had some of that nasty stuff. Dirty-legged slut would do it with a dog if she could find one big enough."

I hit him in the mouth. Knocked all his front teeth out. Think he might have swallowed a couple of them. Got to choking and hacking so bad, I feared for a minute the loose-mouthed jackass might strangle to death right then and there.

Thought that was the end of the disagreement, but about a week later, I walked into class and foot-tall letters written on the blackboard said, "Lookin' fer some damned good fun? See Charlotte Hickerson. La Honda's favorite town pump."

Didn't have to work for the Pinkerton Detective Agency to figure that one out. Found Harvey standing beside our teacher—ugly, one-eyed woman named Hortence Skaggs. Harvey flashed his new snaggle-toothed grin at me like he felt safe. I stomped over and hit him right in the eye. Almost knocked the top of his head off.

Miss Skaggs went to yelping and hollering like a kicked dog. Screamed, "Stop, stop this right now!"

Harvey, silly son of a bitch, came up swinging a long-bladed pocketknife. Thought he would cut me to pieces before I could fish my own pigsticker out of a wadded-up vest pocket. Dumb bastard didn't know any more about knife fighting than he did about the regular kind. Made a lunge at me, and I stabbed him in the side three or four times, so fast he didn't even realize he'd been hurt for a spell.

He kept at me, and went to bleeding pretty good. Soaked his shirt. Some slopped over the waist of his pants. Loudmouthed gal in the mob of kids watching us went to hollering, "Harvey's bleeding. Miss Skaggs, Miss Skaggs, Eli done went and stabbed Harvey."

Well, the poor dumb son of a bitch looked down, saw all that blood, and dropped like an anvil pitched in a well. He got put in bed. I got put in jail.

Marshal Tom Bankston told Mr. Hickerson, "The boy's a danger to the community. I cain't let him out and send him back to our school after he done what he done. I'm trying right now to see if the town can send his murderous ass to the Texas Boys' Reformatory. It's either that, or the penitentiary down at Huntsville. Bet, by God, a little stay in the state pen would teach him to stab folks."

Mr. Hickerson argued that Harvey pulled his knife first. Dumb-assed lawman wouldn't listen. So I sat in my cell, bided my time, and watched everything going on around me for about a week.

Charlotte came by to see me late one afternoon. Unbuttoned her blouse, glanced to make sure the marshal wasn't looking, then grabbed me by my crotch right through the cell door. Jesus, I had to figure out a way to turn the girl off—there were more important fish to fry.

Felt her up as much as I could reach. Then told her to get me a tree limb, at least three feet long and no bigger around than a man's thumb. She brought it to me that night. Wouldn't turn it loose till after I'd spent almost an hour giving her another treatment through the window of my cell.

Soon as the marshal left for his supper the next evening, I used the limb to fish his key ring off a peg on the wall that was situated almost exactly three feet from the last opening in my cell door. Unlocked myself, put the keys back, and blocked the door closed till he'd gone home for the night.

Waited till about eleven o'clock before I made my escape. By then, pretty much everyone in town had turned in and been asleep for at least an hour or two. My getaway that fateful night was the beginning of a murderous journey through hell on earth.

Stopped briefly on the way out of town for a quick trip to the local mercantile. Had little fear of being caught seeing as how the proprietor was a man whose wife had recently died. Reckoned the ancient old fart was so steeped in grief, he'd take little notice of me rummaging through his place of business. I should have done a little more reckoning.

Pried the back door open, and went straight to the gun counter. Picked out a pair of matched, bone-handled '73 Colts, a Winchester Yellow Boy rifle, and a bowie knife. Went through the clothes rack, too. Dressed myself in a whole new set of duds. Nice black suit, white shirt, string tie, boots, and a fine-looking gray felt hat.

Banged around in the dark some before I finally came across a case of .45-caliber ammunition for the pistols and .44s for the rifle. Even found a little metal box full of folding money hidden under the cash register. Hell, there was near five hundred dollars in that box. Couldn't believe anyone was so stupid, or trusting. Not much difference, far as I'm concerned.

Loaded them pistols, and was about to make my final exit when Elroy Cumby, the owner, caught me in the act. Ignorant old bastard surprised the hell out of me. Hard to believe a man that old could hear well enough to be awakened by anything short of the Rapture and the Second Coming.

Dumb son of a bitch stumbled down the stairs from his quarters above the store. Had a double-bit ax in his hands. Yelled, "What the hell you doin' in here, boy?"

I snapped back, "Robbing your store, you bean-counting old bastard." Felt right proud of myself for the snappy comeback.

Suppose he figured to make me feel bad when he said, "Thought you was already locked up fer attempted murder. Well, I'll just take care of you myself, you thievin' little son of a bitch."

Stupid jackass ran at me and swung that ax like he intended to splatter my brains all over the wall. Blade buried up in the countertop less than a foot from where I stood when I jumped out of the way. Pulled one of them pistols I'd just stole, pressed the muzzle against his chest, and shot the hell out of him. Guess I must have fired two or three more times before he dropped to the floor in a heap. Think one round hit him in the eye. Most likely that one killed the ax-swinging idiot. Lucky shot really. If I hadn't been so close, probably would've missed his whole head. Wasn't a real gunfighter at the time.

Noise from the muzzle blast inside Cumby's almost deafened me. My ears rang for a week. Must not have been much more than a group of popping sounds outside. Don't think a single soul in La Honda heard the blasting.

Now, I must admit to feeling right bad about killing ole man Cumby. Hadn't planned it, didn't expect it, and was shocked right to my boot soles when I realized what I'd gone and done. But it's hard to hold back when someone comes at you with an ax. Hell, if I hadn't shot him, that old man would probably have chopped me up like a Sunday fryer.

Bent over his still-warm body and said, "Why'd you do that? Hell, I didn't have any intentions to kill anybody. Stupid old bastard. You've done sealed my fate, sure as Lincoln freed the slaves. God Almighty, but it takes a damned stupid son of a bitch to bring an ax to a pistol fight."

Peeked outside to make certain no one came running my direction. Slipped onto the boardwalk, and strolled down the deserted Main Street. Tried to act like I was on my way to Sunday school, and by God, it worked.

Stopped out front of the Lone Star Saloon. Could hear female laughter and piano music coming from the place. Found a long-legged, dappled gray mare tied to the hitch rail. Animal carried a new saddle, too. Climbed aboard, and ambled out of town like I was simply taking a Sunday afternoon ride in the country.

So, there you have it. In a matter of little more than two years, I'd gone from being the quietly handsome, pious son of a relatively famous traveling preacher, to an extremely dangerous man in my own respect. From the night I shot Cumby forward, damned few men lived who wouldn't eventually know of, and fear, Eli Gault.

Folks have often asked me why the law didn't come gather me up for the hangman. Hell, they tried about every other week or so, it seemed. La Honda's city marshal, Tom Bankston, was the first.

3

"Thunderation commenced."

I rode away from La Honda like the horned devil himself chased me, or maybe it was Pa's ghost. Headed for Waco. No special reason at the time, but I knew for a fact the company there tended to be most agreeable, the weather tolerable, and the town's location on the Brazos River quite beautiful at certain times of the year.

Perhaps more important, I'd met a girl named Millicent Hatcher, daughter of the Reverend Josiah Hatcher, while visiting Waco during one of my father's soul-saving raids some years before. As I remembered, she was a good-looking gal. We'd only been about fourteen years old during my previous visit. Couldn't wait to see her again and try out some of the things I'd learned from Charlotte.

Spent almost three weeks out in the briars and brambles wandering around like Moses in the wilderness. I feared going into all but the most out-of-the-way villages. Chose the smallest possible, most isolated of towns to buy food and supplies.

Practiced every day with my new pistols. Did the majority of my deadly rehearsing with no ammunition in those big Colts, so as not to waste bullets. Damned bullets cost a nickel each. Shooting up a bunch for no good reason was the same as burning cash far as I was concerned. 'Course, I hadn't paid for them ones I'd stole from ole man Cumby, but I couldn't bring myself to squander any. Ain't Christian to be wasteful.

Stopped at a wide spot in the road about a hundred miles north of Uvalde called Bandera. Found me a Mexican leather worker of some repute. No man in Texas made better saddles at the time. He worked me a fine belt and holster for the gun I carried on my hip. Fashioned a second one as a shoulder rig. Told him I wanted at least one of my weapons out of sight.

Got to thinking on the need for more firepower, so, a few days later, I slipped into another one-dog community of stump jumpers called Alta. Stole me a four-barreled derringer I carried in my boot and another Colt I tucked behind my cartridge belt in a kind of cross draw. Felt right comfortable from then on.

Must have made Waco about ten minutes ahead of Marshal Tom Bankston. To tell the righteous truth, I still don't know how that antique son of a bitch found me so quick. Reined in my dappled gray out front of a watering hole called the Capitol Saloon.

Place looked right nice from the street. Figured it had to be cooler at the bar than out in the dust and blowflies. Besides, I was mighty hungry. Figured anywhere men congregated to drink and gamble there had to be food.

Hell, I'd just swallowed down my first mouthful of an ice-cold beer when I heard, "You've led me on a merry chase, Eli. But now it's time for us to head back to La Honda. You've got thievery and bloody murder to answer for, boy."

Glanced up in the mirror hanging behind a bar that'd been shipped by steamer all the way from New York. Leastways, that's what the bartender bragged to this feller standing beside me who'd been nice enough to buy everyone in the place a drink.

Marshal Bankston swayed from foot to foot, five or six steps behind me. Didn't appear agitated, upset, or anything. Just looked bone-tired. Like the poor old fool wanted nothing more in the world than to go home. Sit in his favorite chair. Suck on a glass of cold buttermilk.

Kept at my drink. Refused to turn around. Right cheerful, I said, "Who the hell are you, stranger? Have we met before?"

Bankston drew in a deep breath everyone in the place must have heard. Let all of it out before he said, "I don't have much patience left, Eli. Rode all over hell and gone chasin' you. Fell off my horse the other day and landed in a mesquite bush. Rattler spooked him. Got them damn stickers all in my left shoulder and hand. Ain't in no mood to bandy words with a pup who murdered a good friend of mine."

"Well, I hate to tell you this, sir, but I've never laid eyes on you. Have not the slightest intention of going anywhere with a stranger just 'cause he says he's a lawman from some pissant place in South Texas. Bartender, have you ever seen this man before?"

Couldn't believe it. Feisty bartender gave Bankston a thorough looking over and said, "Nope. Cain't say as I have."

Glanced back into the mirror. Bankston pointed a stubby finger at me and snapped, "Look, boy, I ain't got time for this. I know you're armed. Put your pistol on the bar and step back." He pulled his coattail away from the big Remington on his hip. "Don't want to kill you. But I will, if I have to."

Most of the drunks in attendance that morning had moved to a corner as far away from the rapidly festering disagreement as they could. Bartender took several steps in their direction, but seemed intent on helping me out. He waved a towel at Bankston and said, "Who the hell are you, mister? And why are you pestering this young gentleman?"

Bankston yelped, "He ain't no *gentleman*. Ain't even a *man* yet. Guess you're how old now, Eli? Seventeen, maybe eighteen, if memory serves."

'Course I looked a damn sight older. Didn't notice it till I got to studying on my image in the Capitol's looking glass. One thing them Hickersons did that I liked was eat well. Two years of Miss Estel's cooking, and working like a field hand in her old man's hayloft, had filled me out with a lot of heavy muscle. Done started me a mustache, too. Charlotte said it made me look distinguished. And she liked it for other reasons as well.

Still didn't turn around when I said, "Think you've made a mistake, sir. My name's Henry Moon. Reside over near Tyler. Buy and sell horses for a living. Ain't never been no place named La Honda."

"That's horseshit, Eli. You killed Mr. Cumby, and you're going back for trial and hanging by God. Make up your mind to it, boy." That's when I saw a reflected right hand start for his pistol.

Tom Bankston had no idea what I'd turned into over the more than three weeks he'd been chasing me. Twirled around and had both my weapons up so fast, the remaining poker players between me and him barely had time to get out of the way. Sweet Jesus, glorious thunderation commenced.

I sprayed a curtain of deafening gunfire that scared the bejabbers out of La Honda's marshal and everyone else in the place. Hot lead chewed through the door frame, blasted holes in the front window, and gouged valleys in everything from tabletops to slow-moving sombreros. Hell, it was fast and furious, but horribly inaccurate. Emptied both pistols. Failed to hit Bankston with a damned one of them, near as I could tell.

By the time my single-minded, badge-wearing shadow could figure out what had transpired, I had ducked my head and darted out the back door behind a curtain of black-powder smoke that resembled a fog bank floating low over the Brazos on a summer morning. Ran all the way around the building, jumped on the gray, and high-tailed it away from there.

Headed straight for the Reverend Hatcher's parsonage. Way I had it figured, wouldn't be anyone looking for me in a local preacher's home. Rode around the newly whitewashed house several times before I picked a nice spot in the shade to hide my horse.

Marched up to the door and knocked. Did my best imitation of a young suitor when Millicent's mother answered. Held my hat over the pistol on my hip. Tried my level best to look humble and contrite.

"Yes. What can I do for you, young man?"

"Mrs. Hatcher, do you remember me? I'm Eli Gault. Visited with you and your family some years back when my father, the Reverend Joshua Gault, conducted a week's worth of soul-saving services down by the river. You had us over for supper on a number of occasions. Reverend Hatcher told Pa it was the most successful week's endeavor at soul-saving he'd seen since beginning his ministry."

My efforts at flattery were not without purpose. An empty belly gnawed at the buckle on my pistol belt and rumbled loudly with the least provocation. Tom Bankston had arrived before I'd managed to order anything to eat at the Capitol Saloon. So, my hunger had not abated in the least, and the very sturdy Mrs. Hatcher could easily boast of being one of McLennan County's finest cooks.

She flashed a broad white-toothed smile, opened the screen door, grabbed me by the arm, and pulled me inside. "You come right in here and have a seat, Eli Gault. I've thought of you and your father often over the past few years. Wondered why the two of you hadn't made the circuit and visited with us lately." I knew she'd lead me to her favorite spot in the house—the kitchen table. Woman spent a lot more time sampling her own cooking than she did feeding her imperially thin husband and deliciously buxom daughter.

Dropped my hat on the floor and covered my face with trembling hands. Let out an astonishingly convincing sob and said, "Well, Mrs. Hatcher, one of the reasons I stopped by today was to inform you of my father's foul and unnatural murder a number of years ago near the tiny community of La Honda. Some despicable villain stole into our wagon, slew my father with a shovel, and robbed him of our entire fortune." Tears welled up and flowed freely. I wept like a week-old baby in need of feeding.

Good woman gathered me out of that chair, pressed my face to her ample bosom, and patted my hair whilst I did an impressive bit of acting as the aggrieved child. "There, there, my dear boy. You're in the company of good friends. People who love and will care for you. There's no need to trouble yourself now. Let your heart not be troubled, my son."

'Bout then, Millicent strolled in from her upstairs room and said, "Why, Mother, what in the wide world is going on?"

Mrs. Hatcher led my boo-hooing ass over to her daughter and said, "Millie, you remember young Eli Gault, don't you?"

Snatched a bandanna from the pocket of my coat. Wiped the tears away and held my trembling hand out for the girl. Hell, she had to take it. I didn't give her any choice.

At first, Millicent acted like she didn't recognize me at all, but when I said, "Why, you must recall the time we spent in your swing in the backyard, Miss Hatcher," stars lit up in that gal's eyes. She smiled, bit her lip in an effort to keep from squealing with joy, I'm sure.

She did a little curtsy and said, "Why, yes, I do remember Mr. Gault, Mother. Are you here with your father, Eli?"

Went into my boo-hoo routine again. Startled Millicent. Her mother slapped an ample arm around my heaving shoulders and said, "Don't be so insensitive, girl. The Reverend Gault was murdered by a band of thieving kill-

ers down near La Honda. Young Eli obviously hasn't recovered from the foul deed as yet. Our Christian duty
demands we see to his speedy recovery from this horrid
event. Now, you take a seat, Eli. I've got a nice roast beef
ready, and can see you're in need of a good meal. Nothing
like meat and potatoes to cure what ails you."

Woman fed me till I almost burst. Might as well have
used a shovel. She kept food coming to the table till I
couldn't eat no more. 'Bout the time I finished, Millicent,
who'd been sitting in the chair across the table intently
staring at me, said, "My, my, Eli, why are you carrying so
many pistols."

Hell, I'd meant to take them off before I came in, but
was in such a hurry, the chore had slipped my sustenance-
starved mind. "The heartless skunks what kilt my father
have threatened to do me in as well. My testimony sent
them to prison. But they broke out recently. I've been
moving about ever since in an effort to stay alive. Have
no doubt them murderers will find me eventually. Revenge for any real, or perceived, slight is a potent thing.
The world's a dangerous place, ladies. A man does what
he has to do, even if that means lugging heavy pieces of
iron around all the time."

Mrs. Hatcher looked horrified. Good woman had been
so intent on feeding me, she hadn't bothered to see the
real Eli Gault. She fanned her face and said, "Why, we've
never allowed guns in our house, Eli. Perhaps you'd best
leave them outside while you're here. I'm certain the Reverend Hatcher wouldn't approve."

"Gonna be here long, Eli?" Millicent grinned and fid-
dled with the front of her dress. "Or do you expect those
badmen to appear at just any moment?"

Then it came back to me in quick flashes of heated
memory. That girl always was full of devilment. Her in-
flammatory questions were meant to incite her dithering
mother. It worked. "Do not trouble yourselves, ladies. I'll
take them outside right now, Mrs. Hatcher."

Headed for the gray with Millicent trailing me like a

bloodhound on track. "What are you trying to pull, Eli Gault? I know you're up to no good. Could see it coming when you were here during the revivals. Knew back then you were destined for a bad end."

Shoved the pistols into my bedroll and war bag. When I turned around, Millicent pressed her ample young body against mine like a visiting circus poster glued to a wood fence. Squirmed against my shirtfront till I thought I'd explode. Stuck her tongue in my mouth, then backed away a bit and said, "Don't you remember the good times we had out behind your daddy's tent?"

Pulled her close again. "Of course I remember, Millie. Why do you think I'm here? Men are on my trail, and may be out to kill me. Wanted to visit the most beautiful girl in Texas 'fore I died."

She batted emerald eyes at me and whispered, "Why, Eli, aren't you sweet. Seems you've learned a little about how to better treat girls since your last visit to Waco. As I remember, all you had on your mind behind the Reverend's traveling tent was how fast you could separate me from my underthings."

"Well, I was some younger then. My behavior in such delicate matters has much improved." I was lying like a yeller dog, of course. Charlotte Hickerson had lighted the wick to my lust and the flame burned unabated. The lovely Millicent had no way of knowing my plans yet, but if it proved possible to do what she had already accused me of, I would indulge the growing ache in my smoldering groin for her at the earliest possible instant. Perhaps she read the true feelings hidden in my unrepentant heart, because a quivering smile bled into a thin-lipped scowl for about a second, before she turned and flounced back into the house.

The Reverend Hatcher didn't make an appearance until almost dusk. His countryside circuit of prayer vigils for the lost, ill, and dying took longer than either he or his missus had expected. He heartily shook my hand, and almost wept when I told him of my father's bloody departure from this world at the hands of murderous villains.

Threw a muscular arm around my shoulders, pulled me to my knees, and prayed for almost ten minutes. Finally, he stood and said, "Most appalling, my son. Most appalling. I've known your father for almost twenty year. First time he came through Waco for a visit was back during the War. August or September as I recall. We'd just learned of Vicksburg's fall and the antidraft riots in New York City. Terrible times. His poor wife had passed, bless her soul. Joshua came to town with his four-year-old son. Guess that should make you about eighteen or nineteen now. Don't know why, but the closeness of ages between you and Millie had escaped my memory."

"He never mentioned a prior visit, sir," I said.

"Called on us a second time as well. War had ended a few months before. The hell of Yankee Reconstruction was well under way. Doubt you would remember, but you and Josh stayed here with us for almost six months. We took turns preaching in my church. And when he went out on the evangelism trail, a stop here in our beautiful town took place about every other year. My congregation felt blessed by his close relationship with God."

His revelation came as something of a minor shock. All I'd ever known of the Reverend Hatcher involved a few hazy, barely remembered visits to conduct one of Pa's revivals over the years. Hadn't realized we'd been there so often. Our last visit was the most prominent in my mind. Never forgot the childish infatuation brought on by his beautiful daughter's boldly flirtatious behavior. Got to thinking about my iniquitous intentions concerning Millicent and, for at least five seconds, felt right bad that I'd come up with such low-life purposes. Thank God, those feelings didn't last long.

4

"He's deader'n the handle on a pitchfork."

Being as how I'd arrived on a Wednesday night, my presence was required at the Reverend's weekly prayer meeting. His church was located within walking distance of the parsonage. Congregation gathered me in with open arms. They wept, prayed, and fired the evening's service with loud, heartfelt renditions of all the old hymns. Gave me a warm, homey feeling I'd not had at any time before. Made me feel almost like I'd been there all my life.

Afterward, the Reverend showed me to their nicely done-up guesthouse. The ten-by-ten room was located midway between the Hatchers' home and their barn. I was quite surprised by the dwelling's well-appointed interior. "Why, this is much cozier than sleeping on the ground or under a wagon, sir."

"My son, you are welcome to stay as long as you wish. Please consider yourself one of the family. What I have is yours."

Now, I must tell you in all sincerity that I tried my level best to behave during my stay with those fine folks.

Even made a serious attempt to conduct myself with righteous propriety when around Millicent. And for about three weeks managed to pull it off. But the siren call of sinful deeds kept whispering in my ear, drawing me out of my bed at night to roam the streets and alleys of Waco's rougher areas.

Got to the point where I couldn't wait for night to fall so I could rogue around the saloons, gambling joints, and bars in search of whiskey, poker, and eager women. Over the years, I have come to the belief that such is the fate of young men who do not taste of the world's forbidden fruit until they are almost grown. Then, most can't seem to get enough of anything considered wicked, aberrant, or immoral.

Learned by sheer accident that I had a hidden and untapped talent for poker and other games of chance. Don't have the slightest idea where such an iniquitous flair came from. Pa never gambled. Guess that was about the only sin he didn't indulge in. I'd not so much as picked up a pack of the devil's pasteboards till I walked into the Mustang Saloon one night after sneaking out of bed.

Watched some fellers play poker for about an hour. Sat down with the money I'd liberated from Elroy Cumby's tin box and, before the night ended, tripled my ill-gotten fortune. Hell, winning large piles of other people's money was damn near as much fun as gettin' nekkid with Charlotte. Not quite, but almost.

Ran upon a feller named Diamond Jim Grady one night during my after-dark roguing around. Gambler took a shine to me. Imperially slim and dressed like a dandy of the first order, Jim was a proud son of Mississippi. Physically, he looked like a yard rake clothed in fine silk waistcoats and lace shirtfronts. A smooth baritone voice oozed with the deep Southern sounds of mint juleps served on vast colonnaded porches, fronted with magnolia trees and honeysuckle.

Being the third son in a family of six boys, he realized early on that his chances of inheriting the plantation were pretty damned poor. Not long after his fifteenth birthday passed, Jim hit the trail west, and never looked back.

More than once, he said, "My father doted on Brother Isaac, his firstborn. Boy could do no wrong as far as Pa was concerned. I hated him, and had to get away from Columbus before committing foul and unnatural murder of the Cain and Abel variety."

For reasons unknown, Diamond Jim decided his mission in life was to teach me all he knew about poker. More specifically, all the methods a man might employ to cheat at the game. He showed me how to shave cards with his deluxe ivory-handled card trimmer, and the way to round the corners of selected pasteboards with a similar machine made especially for that particular job.

One night, he handed me a pair of blue-tinted spectacles and said, "Put these on and look at the backs of this deck." Son of a bitch, if those cards weren't marked plain as day in some kind of ink you could only see with his colored goggles. But he warned me not to use the method often, and only when in the company of amateurs.

"Professional gamblers have used this trick for some years now. They'll catch you right quick."

Ole Diamond Jim taught me how to deal seconds, and quick-cut a deck so all the cards stayed exactly where I wanted them. He spent a whole night on how to use just about anything that would reflect an image as a shiner, so I could read the cards as I shuffled and dealt.

My gambler pal gifted me with one hell of an education. Suppose it would have continued if he hadn't got rudely shot to death one night when an equally talented cheat caught him using a shaved deck. Whole enterprise probably wouldn't have amounted to much, but Jim had just about cleaned out everyone at the table over four days of intense poker before a well-known local cardsharp, who made his home in Waco and called himself Rattlesnake McKord, took exception to looming impoverishment.

Personally, didn't need but a few weeks of concentrated play before I learned all about another of poker's nastier negatives that could also get you shot graveyard dead. Bad enough to get caught cheating, but some bastards just hate like hell to lose whether they're being swindled or not. Silly idiots usually can't play worth a damn, but don't seem to know it. Sons of bitches think there ain't nobody on the planet has their skill or knowledge of the game at hand. First feller I had a violent run-in with over my newfound skills was a one-eyed, jug-headed jackass named Davis Meckler.

Two weeks after Jim bit the dust, a full table had been going at it for about three hours when I threw down a ten-high straight and raked in a huge pile of loot. Meckler grabbed at my hand and said, "Goddammit, how many pots does that make for you tonight, boy? Ain't never played poker with anybody that wins the way you do. Must be somethin' going on here as I cain't see."

Leaned back in my chair and eased a hand toward my belly gun. I'd only worked at the gambling trade for a few weeks, but knew it's a deadly business when you start accusing a man of cheating.

I'd also discovered, during the course of my saloon crawls, that there's just nothing like the Bible and Shakespeare for a vocabulary that can confuse hell out of a brush-popping idiot. All it took was a little education and a lot of nerve to really piss one of them off. So I said, "Why, Davis, your uncensored harangue seems tinted with an accusatory ring. Whatever are you implying?"

His head tilted to one side like a dog engrossed in a futile attempt to understand mathematics. "What the hell, are you a-tryin' to insult me, boy? By God, pissants like you should be right careful what they say to a real man." The word man stretched out slow, like he really meant to say, "Far as I'm concerned, you're nothing more'n a scabrous pile of something sticky on my boot sole."

Several of the other fellers at the table pushed their chairs back, stood, and moved to spots along the walls. "Now look what you've gone and accomplished, Davis.

You've startled and alarmed our boon companions. What on earth shall we do for future camaraderie?"

Longer I talked, the redder his face got. Looked for an instant as though his bulbous, blue-veined nose might explode. He made the mistake of leaning toward me when he said, "I've squashed a bushel basket of dung beetles tougher'n you, boy. Stompin' a soft-shelled bug like you is gonna be the easiest thing I've done all week." Then he went for the pistol jammed behind a double-row cartridge belt.

His awkward, leaning-over-the-table position simply wasn't conducive for effective gunfighting. On top of that, he got his gun hand tangled in a pair of loose-fitting braces. By the time he could get his pistol up, I'd already fired four shots and, miracle of miracles, three of them hit him dead center.

Two of those big chunks of lead punched all the way though the man. Sent wood splinters from his chair along with gouts of spraying gore flying across the room behind him. A heavy cloud of blue gray gun smoke hovered around us as though we sat inside an all-enveloping storm.

Could barely see ole Davis as he glanced down at his chest, dipped a trembling finger into one of the bloody holes, and grunted, "Well, I'll just be damned." Pistol slipped from his grasp and loudly thumped when it hit the floor. His gaze came up to me for a second, before he tipped over and landed nose-first on the tabletop. Pile of chips and change splattered out around his face. Blood leaked from the corner of his mouth and stained the green felt.

For a minute or more, the Mustang got so quiet, you could hear mice humping under the floorboards. The acrid smoke from my pistol drifted to a corner of the room as I stood and pushed my chair away from the table.

The bartender, a right nice gentleman named Anson Byers, kind of hopped over, pressed a finger to Meckler's neck, and said, "He's deader'n the handle on a pitchfork." Then he turned to me. "I'd get the hell out of here if I was you, son. Town constabulary don't take well to barroom shootings. Last feller what done one got throwed in jail. Tried and hung within a week."

Scraped all the money left on the table, even some stained with Meckler's blood, into my hat. Snugged the sombrero down on my head and said, "I do appreciate the advice, Mr. Byers. My apologies for the disruption of your evening's business and for any problems this might cause you in the future."

He smiled at my youthful honesty. "Hell, this ain't the first corpse I've had sitting at one of my tables, and probably won't be the last. But like I said before, if it was me, I'd burn boot leather getting away from Waco."

Offered him my hand. He shook it. I said, "Thank you, sir. Hope to one day come back under more pleasant circumstances."

Last thing I heard as I headed for the Mustang's back door was, "You do that, young man."

Fogged it for the Hatchers' guesthouse and packed quickly as I could. Threw everything I owned into my bedroll and war bag. Tiptoed down to the barn. Thought I was on the way to making a right slick getaway when I heard horses thunder up to the front of the parsonage. Soon as I threw my saddle on the gray, someone banged on the front door of the guesthouse.

Got all cinched, loaded up, and ready to run when I heard the rumbling voice of a man I assumed belonged to the town marshal yell, "Eli Gault, we have you surrounded. Come out of the house and turn yourself in. You have one minute, sir. If you are not standing on the porch in that time, I will order my men to commence shooting."

Peeked from the barn door and, sure enough, eight or ten men carrying an array of deadly weapons had the Reverend Hatcher's tidy little guesthouse totally encircled. Waco's lawdog proved good for his word, too. Exactly one minute after his shouted warnings, he gave a signal and the blasting commenced.

Those dumb bastards fired everything they had as fast

as anyone could humanly do it. Only God knows how many pieces of lead they poured into my abandoned hiding place. Struck me as right funny for a time. I went to laughing, and almost forgot I needed to hightail it for the big cold and lonely as quick as I could.

Finally came back to my senses when Mrs. Hatcher ran from the back door of the main house screaming like a gut-shot panther. Poor woman still wore her nightdress, was barefooted, and appeared to have gone totally insane.

She broke through the line of lawmen, screeching at the top of her lungs, and headed for their target's front door. Could still hear her yelling my name as I saddled up and slipped out the barn's back way. Must have been five miles out of town before they realized I'd made my escape.

5

"The most accomplished man killer in Texas."

Took almost a week for me to shake loose from the posse that dogged my trail. Rode around in a big looping circle for three days. Think I finally lost them in the cane breaks about thirty miles out of town up on the North Fork of the Bosque River. Soon as I realized my pursuers had most likely given up the hunt, turned the gray and headed east for the Navasota. Took three more days of sneaking and hiding before I finally felt relatively safe again.

Was in search of a spot to camp, on my sixth day in the briars and brambles, when I came upon a feller who'd already staked out a likely place and had coffee cooking. Not much light left. Dismounted and walked up as close as I felt would be safe and said, in as unthreatening a way as possible, "Evening, sir. Wonder if you might share a cup of that fine-smelling brew you've got on the fire."

Man was hatless, and sat with his back to a sheltering nook between the huge roots of a live oak. Even in the poor glow given off by his dying fire, I could see suspicion etched into a fearsome face. His saddle and other belongings were neatly laid out under a lean-to tarp affair draped over a low-hanging limb. A long-legged black, tied to a bush, munched grass about twenty feet away.

Figured the fellow'd probably send me packing with gunfire chasing behind. Must admit I was some surprised when he said, "Come on in. They's an extra cup there by the pot."

His deep, animalistic voice rumbled and growled at me, but my hunger overcame any hidden threat I might have detected there. Tried my level best not to look anxious as I headed for the warmth of his cook ring.

Squatted, and poured myself a hearty portion of his freshly made belly wash. Stuff was so strong, I think it could've walked from the pot to my cup. Said, "Do appreciate the kindness, sir. I've about worn myself to a frazzle. Been on the move for several days. Haven't had a decent helpin' of up-and-at-'em juice the whole time. Not much in the way of food neither."

My mysterious host pointed to an iron skillet next to the coffee and said, "They's bacon and fried cornpone in that 'ere pan. Throw it to the forest's creatures if'n you don't eat it."

"Sure you don't mind?"

"Done told you how I felt on the matter. Have a bit of something to eat, boy. Feller your age needs considerable more in the way of nourishment than old wolverines like me."

Set to gnawing on his bacon and pone. Hell, I was so hungry, a plate of boiled boot heels would have tasted good. Got down to the last piece of bacon before the founder of the feast spoke again. He rolled himself a cigarette and said, "What's your name, son?"

Had no reason to lie. Didn't know him from Adam so I said, "Eli. Eli Gault. And yours, sir?"

Caught him glaring at me, and reckoned I might have stepped across some kind of invisible line he didn't want violated. But, hell, he'd started it. When he finally said, "Cutter Sharpe," I almost passed out.

Cutter Sharpe was burdened with the rather dubious reputation as one of the most accomplished man killers in Texas. His standing as a consummate gun handler had spread far and wide. If you could find anyone in the state who hadn't heard of him, that person was probably the resident of a graveyard and had been in the ground for a good many years. Way the tales got told and retold, the man eyeballing me while I ate his food had sent more than his share to those same cemeteries.

Grew a sizable bold streak when I said, "Rumor has it you're one of the most dangerous men alive. That true?"

The wary gunman shifted in his seat and chuckled. Sound came from deep inside his chest. He wiped a drooping mustache on back of the hand holding the cigarette and said, "Well, young Eli Gault, you missed the mark by an inch or two. Truth is, I am *the* most dangerous man alive."

Now, that's what I had wanted to say, but thought he might not take well to being described in such a manner. Sought to soften my initial remarks and thereby gain his trust. But since he'd opened that jug himself, I said, "I do appreciate you allowing me your company, Mr. Sharpe. Would you mind if I asked you another question, sir?"

He chuckled again. "You know, I've always admired the ironbound boldness that comes with the stupidity of youth. Ask away, Eli. I'm feeling right sociable presently. And there ain't nobody around this small chunk of woodsy heaven but you, me, and the skeeters on this starless night, so go on ahead and spit it out."

Stood and moved to the side of the fire closest to his resting place. Squatted again to restore his level of comfort. "Can you teach me how to handle a gun, Mr. Sharpe? I do all right, as long as I'm up close. Usually put out as much lead as possible and pray I hit something. My self-taught approach has served me well so far. But I fear the method might be lacking in good judgment should I ever come up against a truly talented gun handler. And given the events of my recent life, I feel your assistance could prove beneficial to my continued existence."

He laughed out loud, coughed, flicked the cigarette into the dying fire, and said, "Damned if you ain't one fast-talking son of a bitch, Eli. Filled my ears up till I don't think you could put any more words in 'em tonight. Might cause my head to crack open." Then he guffawed again. Thought himself right funny, I suppose.

I kept after him. Said, "Didn't mean to appear uppity or too inquisitive, but I'm in dire need, Mr. Cutter. Vengeful men are on my trail at this very moment. Should they catch me, I shudder to think on the fate they might have planned."

Cold blue eyes stared into mine during my hasty appeal. He turned his attention to another raid on a beaded tobacco pouch, and fell into thought until he'd finished rolling a second coffin nail. Finally, he said, "Never had such a request before. Most likely, the solitary nature of my existence prevented appeals like yours in the past. Haven't had the opportunity to consider anything like you've proposed." He sucked in a lungful of smoke, flicked ash toward the fire, and continued. "Tell you what, Eli. Why don't you throw your bedroll down by the fire. We'll both sleep on it. Come tomorrow morning, I'll have your answer. Right now, I'm worn down to a nub. Ain't exactly thinkin' right. Otherwise, I'd of probably shot hell out of you soon as I heard your call to come into camp. A man cain't be too careful these days, you know."

And that's exactly the way the night worked out. Lay in my blanket and wondered what he would do. Even prayed on it some. Figure most folks won't believe it, but that's what I did.

Woke to biscuits baking in a Dutch oven, frying bacon, even scrambled cackle berries. Amazed me that anyone could have eggs out in the middle of nowhere like that. But I discovered in the morning's light a pack animal not previously noticed. Sleek-looking mule appeared to have been loaded with all the necessities for making life as comfortable as possible when a town did not present itself. Vowed to get myself a similar creature at the first opportunity.

Sharpe noticed that I'd come back from the darkness of dreamland. "You ready for some grub, Eli?"

"Yes, sir, I am. Smell from your skillet already lit up my appetite. Think if I don't get some of those biscuits down pretty quick, my stomach might bite a hole in my pistol belt."

Sharpe laughed and kept at his cooking. We ate, and, afterward, I helped him clean up. He stowed away all the pots and pans, then worked both of us a smoke. As we lit up, he said, "Must say, I was intrigued by your proposal last evening, son. Thought on it till deep into the night. Didn't believe there for a spell I'd ever get to sleep." He took a puff and thought some more. "Decided I'd do 'er."

"Can't tell you how much I appreciate your decision, Mr. Sharpe."

"Well, it's a hard life we live these days. They's armies of dangerous men out and about. Time and circumstance has a way of drawing some of us into lives we never intended on living."

"That's exactly what happened," I said. "I'm nothing more than a victim of God-sent circumstance." 'Course that was a bald-faced lie but, like most people my age, I'd been aware of how far you can go on a line of unadulterated bullshit with grown-ups ever since learning how to talk. Just nothing like a pack of lies to make your elders feel good.

"Since I don't know your history, Eli, can't agree or dispute your conclusions. But my own life on the owlhoot trail started as the result of a series of misunderstandings that resulted in killings I had no control over. Since that time, I've been forced into a long list of what civilized society views as atrocities, but were no more than the necessities of survival."

"My story exactly, Mr. Sharpe. Had no idea there were other men who suffered from the same burden."

He crushed the ash of his cigarette on a rock and flicked it aside. "This may well be the Year of Our Lord 1879, but living as we know it, out here on the frontier, is still mean, dangerous, and sometimes downright deadly. Behooves any man who wishes to stay alive to learn the use of firearms. Being as I'm about as good as it gets in such practice, it'd be my pleasure to teach you as much as I can about what I know."

Heavenly days, but I felt as though my chest would fill till it burst with a swelling pride. There I was nothing more than a complete stranger to one of Texas's most prolific murderers, and he had agreed to teach me how to be more effective at the killing trade. My God, but it was inspiring. Felt almost as good as the night I rushed down Pa's aisle and he saved me from eternal damnation. Well, almost as good anyway.

Cutter began his murderous instructions as we traveled a hidden trail that ran from Waco to Nacogdoches. We'd ride a few miles and then stop. While resting our animals, he'd teach. First lesson involved me showing off my version of how to draw and fire. Suffice it to say, my newly made traveling companion was not impressed.

He laid a row of pebbles on a fallen tree. Watched my clumsy efforts with his hands jammed behind a concho-decorated cartridge belt. A crooked frown betrayed his feelings. "You're well enough equipped. Beautiful set of pistols. And you get 'em out and up quick enough, but my God, Eli, you couldn't hit a loaded beer wagon from twenty feet. Hell, you didn't even hit the log, boy," he said, as a heavy cloud of acrid black-powder smoke drifted up our noses and burned our eyes.

"What'd I do wrong?"

"Well, other than a pretty good draw, damn near everything." He placed a comforting hand on my shoulder. "No need to get in such a hurry, son. What a sane man wishes for, more'n anything else, in a gunfight is to get out of the thing alive. Way you accomplish such a heartily desired end is to take your time. As long as you keep your head, you can just about bet that ninety-nine times out of a hundred your opposition is gonna be a hell of a lot more concerned about getting shot and dyin' than you are."

Thought on that one for a spell before I asked, "How's that? Why would my opposition be more anxious than me?"

Cutter pushed his hat back and squinted hard. "Because down deep, where it counts, the average man is a coward. He fears death and sees it coming for him when facing a man he's fully aware just might kill him. Many a sensible feller who stares down the wrong end of one of these .45-caliber blasters can feel the fires of Perdition lickin' at his heels. You just gotta keep your head, son. Deliberate man usually survives to fight again."

I reloaded as he talked. "But there are gunmen in every peckerwood-sized town in Texas these days just looking to make a reputation by killing somebody, anybody who happens by."

He snorted a chuckle. "Aw, hell, Eli, them town gunnies are the blusterin'est, most gutless jackasses of them all. I ain't seen one yet I'd fear, 'less he got behind me. So, what I want you to do is watch me. Count to three and say, go."

Cutter turned kind of sideways to our makeshift target. Far as I could see the odd stance exposed his right side to any potential gunfire. But then it came to me as how he'd narrowed any target his opposition could see. He calmly slipped the leather keeper loop from his pistol's hammer and waited. I did as asked. Said, "Go," and the pistol, strapped high on a bony hip, appeared in a metallic flash. He brought his left hand up to grip the right and used his left thumb to cock the weapon. Faster than I could count them, ole Cutter tore off six shots that all found their mark. Didn't miss once.

"Impressive," I said. "Your method works well at a distance, but what if you're sitting across the table from some dumb ass in a saloon who decides to draw on you."

"Well, hell, if you're less than ten feet away, no reason you shouldn't be able to kill the son of a bitch with damn near no effort at all. Same deal, though. Most men who get sucked into such as you described let their nerve fail them and, before they know what's happened, are staring at the ceiling through dead eyes. Just keep your wits about you."

The lessons continued apace. During the day, Cutter had me shooting at anything and everything. We'd be riding along and he'd point and yelp, "Twig." My job was to hit whatever he indicated as quickly as possible. For the first few days, twigs, stumps, rocks, and even trees were as safe as newly born babes clutched to their mothers' bosoms. I didn't hit a damned thing.

Late on the fourth afternoon, something happened. Can't say exactly what, but everything he directed my attention toward got blasted to bits. "See. You've relaxed," he said. "The gun's becoming a part of you. One-handed shootin's turning into nothing more'n second nature. But you still need to adopt my two-handed approach when afoot. Helps you shoot quick and accurate."

We rode, stopped, lounged beside the trail, burned so much powder that I'd shot up more than two hundred rounds in less than a week. Cutter said, "Most men don't fire a box of shells a year through a pistol. Rifle maybe. Hunter might shoot up that much in a shotgun, but handguns, not a chance. You're way ahead of the game, boy."

At night, he made me take my weapons down to their essential parts. Had to oil and clean every spring, screw, and individual piece. Afterward, he always inspected them. Said he learned the necessity of such discipline riding with Quantrill and the James boys up in Missouri during the War of Yankee Aggression.

We arrived in Nacogdoches after a week on the trail. Cutter had a serious thirst by then, and decided we should take our leisure in the Boar's Breath Saloon, a watering hole he favored above several lesser places along the town's main thoroughfare.

"Cooler in here," he said as we dismounted. "Big room has higher ceilings and a Mexican feller who hand-cranks some fans that are all hooked together with leather straps. Downright homey for fellers like us."

He pushed through a set of ornately carved batwings. I followed him inside. Headed for a table in a corner as far from the entrance as you could get without sitting in the alley. He said, "Never sit near the front of a place like this. Try to find a spot as close to the back door as you can. That way you can see who's comin' at you and, if necessary, make a quick exit."

"Why not sit up front?"

He glanced over and eyeballed me like I was a small child and said, "Too easy for someone to fire from the street before you can see 'em. Hell, I had a friend who was playin' poker at the second table of the Bull's Head down in Gonzales. Feller he'd exchanged words with at some point stood behind the batwings and shot him from outside on the boardwalk. Bastard used a long-barreled shotgun. Blew my compadre's whole head off. Nothing left but the stalk of bone holding it up. You just never know, Eli. Always best to play safe."

A hard-looking woman who must've fancied herself quite the beauty strolled over to our table and said, "You boys drinkin' or lookin' for female companionship this fine summer day?"

She leaned over and gave us a long view down the front of her shabby, spangle-covered blue dress. Rough ole gal had some nice ones on her. Didn't mind showing them off either. Got the impression she'd worked in far nicer joints than the Boar's Breath.

Cutter's tone remained pleasant but firm when he said, "We're drinkin' right now, darlin'. Perhaps the other at some later time."

Gal frowned and headed for the bar. "Suit yourself, cowboy." She brought a bottle, two glasses, and some cigars back to the table, glanced at me, winked, and said, "You've never had any as good as mine, mister. I might be occupied later. Sure you don't want to ride the tiger right now?"

I said, "No, thank you, miss. I'll sit with my friend for a spell."

As saloons go, the Boar's Breath wasn't bad. Not as nice as some in Waco, but not a dump either. We nursed the bottle along, puffed on our cigars, and were having a right pleasant, relaxing afternoon until a feller who looked like a bad dream come to life stepped inside. I'd noticed the odd-looking gomer as he peeked over the batwings before making his dramatic entrance.

Started to mention his presence to Cutter, but he pulled his hat down and said, "I seen 'im. Bounty-huntin' bastard named Spook McCain."

"Is he after you?" I asked.

"Damned if I know. Could be. They's posters out on me all over the state. Depending on where you're from, I'm worth a thousand dollars in Comanche County, or five thousand down in Bexar."

Spook McCain took one step inside the saloon and stopped. Dressed from head to foot in black, he also wore a silver-studded pistol belt and hatband to set off the dark nature of his attire. A matched brace of bone-handled Colts was worn backward under a long frock coat. The contrary arrangement of his weapons reminded me of an illustration I'd seen on the cover of a penny dreadful that purported to be the actual person of Wild Bill Hickok. Boys in school in La Honda handed that book around until it fell apart.

Room fell silent as McCain took two more steps in our direction. Heard the pleasantly musical ring of his solid silver spurs. He stopped again, planted his feet, and pushed his coattails backward. A steely-eyed gaze landed on Cutter and me.

Made ever so slight a move to stand, but Cutter leaned back in his chair and hissed, "Hold still, son. Don't move. Let me handle this." His right hand went to the grip of his belly gun. Opened my jacket, and leaned on the table where I could get at my shoulder rig.

As the bounty hunter, who bore the appearance of a dead undertaker, strode across the barroom of the Boar's Breath, tipplers scurried to the door like whipped dogs. A handful headed for the corners and appeared willing to suffer whatever by way of flying lead might befall them just so they could bear witness to the proceedings.

By the time McCain had jingled his way over to within a few steps of our table, I had my shoulder-holstered hideout in hand and was ready to shoot hell out of the cadaverous-looking bastard if he made the wrong move.

In a voice that sounded like the man gargled horseshoe nails every morning upon arising, McCain said, "They's some irate rich folks down San Antone way will pay a heap of gold coin for your hide, Sharpe."

Cutter grinned and said, "So I hear."

"You done went and killed a state senator. A true hero of the Republic. Old bastard fought at San Jacinto with Houston. Man cain't do crimes of such depravity and git away with 'em, 'less someone like me comes lookin' for him."

"That a fact," my friend replied.

"Natural goddamned fact. One of them kinda facts you can only find in books writ by fellers with college edications."

Cutter really opened the box when he said, "You intend on taking me back to San Antone, Spook?" He didn't wait for a reply. "Think you're good enough to get out of here alive?"

The cadaver's eyes blinked real fast several times before he said, "Hell, Sharpe, I been quicker'n you for more years than this pup with you has been alive."

Well, he'd brought me into the conversation, so I snapped, "Don't bet your life on it, you ugly bag of pustulous shit. I think between the two of us, we can kill you dead times four. When the smoke clears, folk here'bouts will be able to use your sorry ass as a boat anchor. Decision you have today is whether you think it's possible to git back to the boardwalk alive."

A crooked, rotten-toothed smile creaked across McCain's face. "Spunky little shit, ain't you, boy. Gonna take great pleasure killin' hell outta both of you."

Must admit while I had a serious eyeball on Spook McCain's every move, or at least I thought I did, both the man's hands filled with pistols like blue-spiked lightning during a cyclone. Guess he must have thought he could kill me and Cutter at the same time. He had a small problem, though. Cutter Sharpe was just about a shade-and-a-half faster.

First shot fired came from Cutter. Blast from his pistol shocked the hell out of me. Confined space of the bar made his pistol sound like a cannon going off. I'd only heard a weapon fired inside a building once before. Damn near deafened me in my left ear. Cutter's slug hit McCain in his upper left chest and knocked him slightly sideways. Caused his aim to fail. McCain's first shot was directed at me, and sent a heavy block of burning lead so close to my ear, I thought for a second I heard angels singing.

I got my hideout up and into action just as Spook fired a second round, which smacked the tabletop and ricocheted into the ceiling. Thumbed off four shots in response, while Cutter kept pumping lead in the ugly killer's direction. Between the two of us, we hit McCain at least four times. Under the circumstances, it should be understandable that some of our shots went wild. Midway through all the gun smoke and thunderation, a feller in one of the corners yelped like a kicked dog and hit the batwings running.

As quickly, and as brutally, as the action began, it ended. Spook McCain staggered sideways a few steps, dropped one of his pistols, and slumped onto a table near the front window. He rolled onto his back, somehow got himself erect, and stumbled for the door. His gun went off one more time and blew a hole in the floor beside his foot. He made a grab for the top of the batwing, missed, and fell face-forward onto the boardwalk.

Cutter holstered his weapon and said, "Didn't think the son of a bitch was ever gonna die."

"He could still be alive," I said.

"Sweet Jesus, I hope not. Be something of a novelty if he was to stand up and start walking again. Maybe you should go over and put one in his brainpan—just to be sure he's dead."

Hell, I was stunned. "You want me to walk over there and shoot him again?"

He laughed, stood, and said, "Hell, boy, don't you know when someone is kidding? Come on, Eli. Let's get the hell out of here. Don't know what kind of law's working the town these days."

We headed for the street. Had to step over Spook McCain's oozing corpse. Several of our slugs went all the way through the man's body. Saw at least two nasty holes in back of his long black coat.

Thought we'd made our escape, but I'd just put my foot in the stirrup when someone behind us said, "Hold up there, boys. We need to talk a spell." Dropped my reins, turned, and saw an impressive-looking gentleman wearing a badge. His double-barreled coach gun was menacingly pointed in our direction. Men armed in an equally deadly manner stood on either side of Nacogdoches's town marshal.

Heard Cutter hiss, "Shit. Hoped we'd make it to the woods. This ain't good by a damn sight. Whatever you do, don't tell 'em your real name, Eli." And that's how I became even better known to the misinformed as Henry Moon, and some folks mistook Cutter Sharpe for a feller he called Jackson Pike.

6

"Move and I'll put one in your brain."

I'd never been in a *real* jail before, but must admit that John Pinckney Young had a right nice one—much nicer than La Honda's chicken coop. Should also confess that deep down, I actually liked being in jail. As you can imagine, the experience had a certain familiarity about it. At least for the first few days.

Thought that odd circumstance over at some length, and decided as how people tend to be comfortable with what they know. Came to the conclusion that being the only son of Joshua Gault was as close as a body could get to a seventeen-year term down at the Huntsville State Penitentiary.

Marshal Young put Cutter and me in separate cells. Said we might be there a spell before the circuit judge came through. Floors got swept every day. Young made us prisoners do the job, but they did get swept. Our bedding tended to be clean and lacking in the insect neighbors usually found in such places. Food was so tasty, I looked forward to the meals. Deputy named Jonas Horn told me a local lady cooked the stuff. Best I'd had since leaving the Hickerson household. Only thing could have made my stay any more enjoyable would have been Charlotte's passionate company every night.

Young even expressed some degree of understanding about our predicament. Day he locked us up, the man stood outside our cells and said, "Hell, fellers, I do appreciate why you killed him. McCain was known all over this part of Texas as a dangerous man. Type who'd shoot you dead if money could be made by your dying. But I can't have bloody shoot-outs that result in dead bodies and wounded folk right in the middle of town. Personally, I have no doubt Judge Grimsley will find that your actions were self-defense. Until then, just relax and enjoy your stay."

If my memory hasn't failed me completely, I think we'd been locked up for about a week when I let Cutter know that the marshal and his men had failed to find the four-shot derringer hidden in my boot. Happened one night after my fourth or fifth run-in with one of Marshal Young's deputies. Cutter's eyes lit up like I'd just handed him a five-pound sack full of high-grade California gold dust.

"You mean to tell me you've had that weapon all this time and are just now telling me?" he hissed between the bars.

Didn't have a good excuse for my oversight. So I just said, "Yeah. Figured we might want to let the situation calm down a bit before trying anything. Didn't count on circumstances like what's been going on, though. That's understandable, ain't it, Cutter?"

"Might be understandable, but you shoulda told me so I could have decided what to do and made plans to accomplish our deliverance from this god-awful place."

That's just about exactly what I expected him to say, and the very reason why I'd kept the tiny gun's existence a secret. Hell, we had three squares a day coming, didn't have to do nothing but sweep our cells out and make our cots in the morning. Then we could lounge around, sleep, whittle, play checkers, read, or do any damned thing we wanted. It bordered on paradise.

The marshal and most of his deputies were nice folks. They treated us extremely well—except for one of them. Feller named Clinton Turnbow worked nights and, for reasons known only to God and Clinton, the man hated me from the first moment we set eyes on each other.

He always relieved the day deputy at about five o'clock in the afternoon. Left me to myself early on. Then, first time nobody was around, he started ragging on my locked-up ass. Loved to pick at me. Always throwing something awful into my cell. Hadn't been there but two or three days when he jammed his arm through the bars and dumped a big pile of horse apples all over my clean floor. Good God, they smelled somethin' awful. To my thinking, seemed as though he'd been aging them meadow muffins till some-one like me showed up to torment.

Cutter yelled, "You stupid son of a bitch. Get that shit outta here. Odifirizes the whole damned jail."

Turnbow slammed the door that separated the cell block from the sheriff's office. Through the slot used by the jailers to look in on us, he said, "You want them smelly fritters gone, pick 'em up and dump 'em out the window. Or you can just let 'em lay there and stink." Then he went to laughing like an inmate at some insane asylum.

We searched our cells and Cutter came up with a piece of newspaper he found under his mattress. I busted a chunk of wood off my bunk and managed to scrape most of the foul-smelling stuff up and dump it outside. But, hell, the pungent aroma lingered.

Badge-wearing son of a bitch woke me up again about two hours later. He'd placed a bucket full of water and a mop inside my cell. Said, "Git your lazy ass outta bed and clean that stink up. Would't want the sheriff to think you had to do your business on the floor now, would we?"

Laid in my bunk and said, "Clean it up yourself. You did it."

He glared at me between the bars. Jammed his key into the lock and said, "If I have to come in there, boy, I'll kick your ass so hard, you'll have to unbutton your shirt every time you go to the shit house. Whuppin's gonna commence at the count of three. Once I turn this key, it'll be too late. Serious ass kicking will definitely follow."

Cutter sat up and said, "Leave the boy alone."

Turnbow didn't even look my compadre's direction when he said, "Go back to sleep, Pike, or you just might be in for the same treatment."

My friend got the deputy's attention when he snapped back, "Come in my cell, you stupid son of a bitch, and you'll be ready for a cold slab down at the undertaker's tomorrow mornin'. Just bring that key on over here, open my cell door, and see what happens."

A mocking chuckle escaped Turnbow's throat. "Be careful, old man. I just might take you up on that invitation. You mighta been somebody 'fore we throwed you in that cell, but now you're just another raggedy-assed, cellar-dwelling piece of sorry trash, unfit to live amongst decent folk." Then he turned back to me and started counting. "One."

I waited till "two" passed his lips before I dragged out of bed and went to mopping. Got everything scrubbed down and smelling good in less than ten minutes. He made me back away from the door before he opened it and reached inside for his bucket. He swung the mop around on his way out. Handle whacked me upside the head. Raised a goose-egg-sized knot over my eyebrow. Could hear him laughing behind the safety of the office door.

Was nursing my aching head when Cutter said, "Watch him, Eli. Bullies like Turnbow can make your life miserable. They'll hurt you if you ain't paying attention. But don't worry, son, his time is coming. I'll see to it."

Well, I kept my eye on the tormenting bastard, but for four nights in a row, he seemed to think of a new form of hell to dump on me. Last time he pulled one of his pranks was when I showed Cutter the derringer.

Snapped awake soaking wet at about two in the morning of our seventh day in captivity. Turnbow stood outside my cell door, laughing like something crazed. He held a wooden bucket by his side and said, "Took me a week to save all that piss up. Hope you like it, you son of a bitch."

Whatever he threw on me sure enough smelled bad, but I'm not certain the liquid was exactly what he claimed. 'Course it could have been. Knowing the wicked turn of the man's mind, anything was possible.

Cutter hopped off his bed, and painted the air blue with a stream of curses that would have sent any decent woman to the safety of a fluttering fan and a hasty exit. Turnbow stomped out, laughing again.

Soon as I told Cutter about the derringer, and we'd talked it over, he said, "Give it to me, Eli."

Looking back on the whole situation, I'd probably have been better served by not mentioning the weapon to a man like Cutter. Don't think I would have used it the way he intended, but then you just never know how things will work out when someone starts in with the kind of torturous behavior Turnbow enjoyed.

Handed my friend the derringer through the bars between our cells. That's when he admonished me again for not keeping him informed that I had the gun.

He checked the loads. Even took each shell out and looked it over to make sure there was nothing amiss. Then he said, "Here's what we'll do. Next time that son of a bitch comes in to check on us, you call him over to your door. Since he'll have to walk right past me, we'll have him in a corner where there won't be any place for the bastard to run or hide. After that, leave it to me."

Didn't have long to wait. Turnbow had a habit of looking in on us at least once every hour. But he enjoyed persecuting me so much that he'd be in about every ten minutes most nights. He'd stroll in and spit at me, stand by the door and curse me, or talk in the foulest terms about my mama. Hell, just anything to make me miserable and leave the impression that something worse lay in the future.

Sure enough, fifteen or twenty minutes after he'd soaked me down, the big bastard slammed the door against the wall and strode directly to my cell. He banged the jail's big key ring against the bars and said, "Wake up, goddammit. Scum like you don't deserve to get a good night's sleep. Once your trial's over, and the good citizens of Nacogdoches have sent you to the penitentiary, I'm gonna make sure some of my friends down at Huntsville know you're coming. They'll give you a real sweet welcome, sonny boy."

Rolled over in my cot and said, "Ain't no jury in Texas gonna convict us for killing Spook McCain. Even Marshal Young said we'd probably be acquitted. Why don't you leave us the hell alone before we're forced to hurt you, Turnbow."

Smile bled from his face like water running off a tin roof. He growled, "Hurt me? Did you say you might hurt me?"

Ignorant son of a bitch moved right up against my cell door. That's when he heard Cutter say, "Move and I'll put one in your brain, you stupid bastard."

Big deputy cut his eyes toward my partner's cell, and found himself looking into the bottom of four barrels of potential death. Cutter stood in the corner nearest me. Had his arm through the spaces between the bars. Pistol no more than two feet from Turnbow's enormous thick skull.

"Now," Cutter hissed, "turn to your right and carefully hand them keys through the bars to young Mr. Moon. You make even the slightest move toward that pistol on your hip, and four pieces of lead's gonna make your head into a water trough. Let him hand them to you, Henry, then get his gun."

Soon as the bothersome jackass slipped the key ring into my hands, I reached over and snatched his pistol out of its holster, opened my cell, and with his own weapon, motioned the belligerent deputy to a spot against the wall. He had his hands in the air. I do declare he had the appearance of a man in the throes of advanced malaria.

Cutter came out of his cell like a teased tiger. He grabbed the deputy's gun out of my hand, jumped up in the terrified man's face, and snarled, "Well, now, wonder just how brave you're feeling right this instant, Clinton. You want to throw a bucket of piss on my friend again? Dump piles of horse dung in our cells? That what you'd like to do right now?"

Turnbow shook so bad, I thought he'd collapse right in front of us. He almost cried when he said, "Look, fellers, I was just funnin'. You know how it is. Middle of the night. Nothing to do. Just trying to entertain myself so I could stay awake. Didn't mean nothin' by it."

Cutter shoved the pistol barrel so deep into the quivering man's gut, I could only see about half of it. He was almost nose to nose with my tormentor when he snapped, "Get your big ass into that cell before I completely lose my temper and kill the hell out of you."

Turnbow's feet couldn't have touched the floor. Man must have jumped damn near ten feet. Snatched the door closed behind him and said, "Won't yell, won't make no outcry till you boys is out of town. You can trust me. I swear it. Bang my head on the wall and say you knocked me out. Won't even mention you had the derringer."

Cutter said, "Where's our belongings? Our animals? That horse and mule mean a lot to me. And if they's one thing missing from my property, I'll come back here and kill the whole damned lot of you."

"Traps, saddles, and such is on the floor out yonder in the office. Guns in the rack on the wall behind the marshal's desk. Nothing's gone missing, I swear. Horses and the mule's at Turner's Livery."

"Where's that," I snapped.

A shaking finger pointed the direction as he said, "Turn right when you go out the door. At the end of Main Street. Wake ole man Turner up. Tell him Clinton Turnbow sent you. He'll let you have your animals, no questions asked. I swear it."

Over his shoulder, Cutter said to me, "Henry, look in

the office and see if he's telling the truth. Check everything before you come back. Make damned sure our weapons are out there."

Sure enough, all our stuff was stacked up in one corner of the office. I called out that everything seemed in place, and was searching through the pile when I heard several muffled "thumps" from the cell block that were loud enough to really get my attention.

Ran back inside to find Cutter where I'd left him, but with a pillow draped over his gun hand. Clinton Turnbow lay slumped into my cot. Most of his head had slid down the wall behind him in a gooey mass of blood, bone, and brains.

"Damn, Cutter, I thought you'd decided to let him live."

He dropped the pillow and headed for the door. "Changed my mind," he mumbled. "Bastards like him don't need to breathe our air."

We grabbed all our guns and gear. Headed for the livery fast as we could hoof it under the load. Sun was just before getting up, and old man Turner's day had already begun. He didn't seem the least bit surprised when we told him Turnbow sent us.

Cutter could be right sociable when such behavior was required. He and the old man cussed, and discussed, like lifelong compadres as we got saddled and loaded.

And while he might not have been taken aback by our early morning appearance, Turner did seem a bit inquisitive when he said, "Marshal Young decide to drop the charges agin you fellers?"

Cutter didn't even look up from his efforts when he said, "Yep. Said the way he figured it, innocent boys like us should be thanked for doing the State of Texas a service by rubbing out worthless scum like Spook McCain."

Turner sounded like a Baptist deacon when he replied, "Well, amen to that."

As we climbed into our saddles, Cutter said, "And you know, my friend, I thank God Almighty there's still fine, upstanding men like Marshal John Pinckney Young around who realize the justifiable nature of misunderstandings such as ours." He leaned down, shook the old man's hand, then handed him a ten-dollar gold piece. "You make it a point to thank him for us next time you see him. Would you do that for me?"

The old stableman's eyes misted up when he said, "For this amount of money, I will definitely do that for you, sir. Be assured I will. May God protect you on your journey, gentlemen. Hope to see you again in the near future."

Hadn't got far when Cutter chuckled and said, "Sweet Jesus, never forget, son, all it takes to fool some people is a little money and a shovelful of bullshit."

From the stable, we headed east, but had only gone four or five miles when Cutter turned us north in a big half circle that pointed us toward Fort Worth. He said, "We'll push this as hard as we can till we get to Hell's Half Acre. Young won't ever find us there. Fact, nobody will be able to find us there."

Somewhere along the trail to Fort Worth, I came to realize exactly what had occurred when my partner murdered Deputy Marshal Clinton Turnbow. He'd made me party to a killing not of my choosing.

Hell, there's no doubt I hated the dead son of a bitch, but he was a lawman. Even as young, and stupid, as I had to admit to being, I knew that lawdogs tended to be cultish in their devotion to one another. Every badge-carrying bastard in the state would be on our trail now. And given the slightest chance, one of them would kill us both graveyard dead. Got to figuring that if me and Cutter lived another month, we'd be the luckiest men in Texas.

7

"The hell you say."

At first, I felt sure we'd make our destination in a week or so, but Cutter had other plans. Once we got out into the unpopulated countryside, he zigged and zagged so much I couldn't tell which direction we were headed about half the time.

We'd been running hard for three days when I said, "Sweet Jesus, my ass is killing me, Cutter. We've been in the saddle from daylight till dark ever since we rode out of Nacogdoches. We ever gonna slow down a bit?"

He threw me a smoldering glance over his shoulder. "John Young ain't no fool, boy," he said. "Man's been on our trail since the minute he found Turnbow's pea-sized brain splattered all over that cell wall."

"You really think he'd follow us this far from his home base?"

"Hell, we haven't really gone that far yet."

"Must have been at least a hundred miles, hasn't it?"

He chuckled and shook his head. "I can tell you ain't been at this runnin' and hidin' game long, have you, Eli?"

"Well, no," I said. "But that don't make me an idiot. Way we've been going at this, we shouldn't be far from Fort Worth by now."

"We ain't even halfway there yet. Ran in ever-widening circles the first two days. Then headed south for a spell, north for a while, even doubled back to within ten miles of Nacogdoches at one point."

"Christ on a crutch, Cutter. At this rate, it'll take us a month to get to Fort Worth."

All he said in reply was, "Just about."

On the fourth day, he finally let up some. Stopped on a hill, and sat for almost two hours watching our back trail through his long glass. Finally, he said, "Think we lost 'em, Eli. Can't see any movement behind us. I can usually spot the most careful trackers around. Could be as how Marshal Young might be determined, but maybe he ain't very smart. Just as well. I'm in the mood for a night in a hotel bed. Want me a skin-singer of a bath. Visit with a hot-blooded bawdy woman. Maybe gamble some. How 'bout it, son?"

"Sounds good to me."

"Well, then, we'll head for Six Points. One-horse, one-saloon, one-hotel town where there shouldn't be anyone who'll know us. Get us a good scrubbin', visit the ladies, play a little poker, drink a tubful of spider-killer if the saloon's still up and running. Last time I rode through the place, damned near everything there looked on the verge of blowing away."

Said, "I don't have no money, Cutter. Not a red cent. Marshal and his deputies took my whole poke when we checked into his jail. Didn't think to go through his desk drawers for it when we left."

"Don't worry, son. I've got plenty. Old trick you need to learn. Convert everything to paper. Slit the lining of your favorite coat. Put the money inside, sew 'er back up for emergencies. Usually carry at least a thousand dollars with me. Hell, I've got money hid in virtually every piece of clothing I own. Probably hauling three or four thousand around most times."

Struck me as downright odd that anyone would have that much cash on them, or tell about it. "Risky behavior, isn't it?" I asked.

Cutter laughed so hard he almost fell off his horse. "What the hell's so funny, old man?"

He reined up and went into a coughing fit. When he was finally able to speak, he said, "Who in hell's gonna try and rob Cutter Sharpe—one of the deadliest pistoleers in all of Tejas? Anybody that stupid should end up deader than Davy Crockett."

"Not everyone knows you by sight, Cutter. If those boys back in Nacogdoches had recognized you, bet they'd of hung your old ass on the spot."

That forceful argument set him to laughing again. "God, but you're right, Eli. Guess the only folks what would know a gunman like me would have to have seen my face on a wanted poster. But, hell, most of them sorry handbills don't have a likeness of any kind, just a bad description. And them what has pictures don't look nothing like me. Hell, next time we run on one we'll steal it. Some of 'em is funnier'n a three-legged mule tryin' to pull a buggy."

Six Points turned out like a host of other backwater Texas towns. Half a dozen rugged roads crossed each other in the town's rapidly deteriorating square, then fanned out to finer and more prosperous settlements all over the state. Place was about as big as the little end of nothing whittled to a sharp tip.

Years before, those six thoroughfares brought cowboys on their way home from cattle drives, traveling drummers, gamblers, thieves, and killers in search of a place to sleep and refuge from the trail. Now, building after building appeared empty and abandoned to the vagaries of the harsh local weather.

But wonders of wonders, the saloon and hotel appeared shabby but prosperous, and seemed to be going full blast. Looked like a teakettle about to explode. Closer we got to the center of town, the more colorful wagons, horses, and people we came upon. They were strung out all around the town square. Hell, it was a traveling circus.

Pa and I'd run across such spectacles a time or two in our extensive journeys. The one in Six Points was larger than most. A perambulating menagerie of strange beasts of a type and variety I'd only seen once or twice in my short life were corralled in rope enclosures at every blink of the eye. I saw elephants in one large pen and a pair of camels in a second. Even had some striped animals that resembled black-and-white mules in another.

We passed a wagon full of African lions. Leastways, that's what the sign on the side of the trailer said they was. Biggest cats I'd ever seen. Feller sporting bushy chin whiskers led a monstrous black bear down the street on a chain. Elaborately painted sign on top of a tiger cage identified the bodacious spectacle as COLONEL JOSIAH THOMPSON'S CIRCUS, CARNIVAL, AND EXOTIC ANIMAL SHOW—SEE THE MOST BEAUTIFUL WOMEN IN THE WORLD.

The part about the females proved somewhat accurate. All kinds, types, and sizes of the fairer sex strutted around in various states of undress. Some of them might have been recognized as semibeautiful; a few bordered on pretty. One right nice-looking ole gal was covered, head and foot, with tattoos. Another sported a stringy beard that came all the way down to her waist.

At the time, I supposed that under a tent, and at a distance, it would have been difficult for most folks to tell whether any of those females were *beautiful* or not. Back in those days, most men didn't much care about beauty. Especially if the woman was only partially dressed. And if completely nude, any female available could be ugly enough to make a freight train take a dirt road and it wouldn't matter a whit.

What we'd happened upon by accident was a total wonderment. Couldn't believe my eyes. Don't think Cutter could either. For all his worldliness, he looked like a flabbergasted farm boy on his first trip to town.

I heard him mutter, "Well, damnation. Don't this beat all you've ever witnessed, Eli?"

We tied up at the hitch rack in front of the Six Points Hotel. Went directly to the desk. Place had seen far better days. Interior and exterior needed a heavy coat of paint, or at the very least a wet mop. But appearance didn't mean much that night. Run-down lodge bustled with activity. Gamblers, bootleggers, thieves, and every other sort of riffraff imaginable had followed Colonel Thompson's extravaganza like buzzards circling a bloated corpse. There was money to be made, suckers to be fleeced, and loose women to be had at every turn of the head.

Snippy-acting desk clerk saw us coming. He held up a limp-wristed hand that fluttered like a dying dove and said, "Sorry, gentlemen, but we don't have so much as an empty closet tonight."

Cutter looked right put out. "Mean to say you don't have nothin'?" He pointed off to his left. "How 'bout them billiard tables. Know you've got two of 'em back yonder in that room. Hell, we'll sleep on them."

"Sorry, they're taken, too."

"We'll sleep under 'em."

"Not a chance, sir. By midnight, there won't be so much as an available inch of floor space either. I fully expect to have men, and women, sleeping in the halls, here in the lobby, even out on the boardwalk."

"What about a bath?" I asked.

Pencil pusher gandered around the room like he teetered on the verge of collapse from boredom and said, "Got five freshly hired employees carrying water as fast as they are humanly able, and there's at least a three-to-five-hour wait for a bath. Biggest night in Six Points in more than two years, gentlemen. A bath is most likely out of the question until sometime tomorrow morning. Ten o'clock at the earliest."

Cutter was about as flummoxed as a man could get. "The hell you say."

"Absolutely, sir. The hell I certainly do say. To repeat myself for about the third time, there's not a square foot of empty space available until tomorrow night when these fine *theatrical* folk have vacated the premises." Clerk said "theatrical" like he had something about the size of a guinea egg stuck in his throat he needed to hack up and spit onto his countertop.

Tired to the bone, my partner got right impatient. Reached over the counter and grabbed the hotel feller by the shirtfront. Cocked his head to one side, nailed the ill-humored gomer with a snarl, and snapped, "Do you know of any place out of the weather we might be able to get a bath and put up for the night?"

About then, I think the hotel's most visible if somewhat unfriendly representative realized he had a man not to be trifled with standing in front of him. He went to fumbling with his register when Cutter dropped him. He blinked real fast for a spell while rivers of sweat poured into a greasy collar.

"W-w-well, sir. I-I think I might be able to help you. There is a lady who lives about two miles west of town who takes boarders. Keeps clean rooms, serves meals, and provides baths for a single reasonable price. She should have something available." He waved a limber arm at the seething crowd around us and added, "I don't think any of this rabble wants to reside that far from whatever the night might bring by way of action."

"You got a name for us?" I asked.

"Mrs. Scott, my good sir. Mrs. Hanna Scott. A fine, upstanding lady. Can't miss her place. It's a neatly cared-for two-story home. Sports a white picket fence and a sign out front. I would be most pleased to write an introductory note informing her that I sent you along."

We took the much-put-upon clerk's short missive and headed out of town. Mrs. Scott's boardinghouse appeared exactly as described. In one corner of her grass-covered yard, behind the picket fence, a huge magnolia sported massive blossoms that saturated the entire area in a sweet and

pleasant perfume. A white-haired, grandmotherly-looking
woman occupied one of the half-dozen rockers decorating
a deep porch across the entire front of the home. She
waved when we stopped, stood, and invited us inside.

Cutter handed the well-fed lady our introduction and,
as we stepped onto her porch, she said, "Gentlemen, you
look plumb tuckered out. There are hot baths available.
Walk down the hallway, straight through the house. Tubs,
towels, and such are waiting on the back porch. While you
bathe, I'll prepare supper and have it on the table when
you're cleansed and feeling better."

We thanked her, and followed as she ushered us to
our baths. My God, it'd been a spell since I'd spent any
time sitting in a hot tub of soapy water. Pitched the
clothes I wore into the trash. They still reeked of whatever Turnbow threw on me. Pulled a fresh suit from my
saddlebags after the best soak I could remember. Went to
Mrs. Scott's table in a state of virtual slobber from the
tasty aromas exuded by country-fried chicken, roasted
potatoes, and the most delicious turnip greens I'd ever
tasted. Served 'em with a stack of biscuits, each the size
of a blacksmith's fist, and flour gravy. One helluva fine
meal.

Cutter finished his last bite, dropped the fork on his
plate, patted an extended stomach. "That was the finest
feed I've had in ages, Mrs. Scott. My heartfelt compli-
ments."

"Why, thank you, sir. If you liked the chicken, you're
gonna love breakfast come morning. Six scrambled eggs
fresh from my own henhouse, six flapjacks, a slab of bacon, and enough coffee to float a horseshoe."

I said, "Sounds mighty good to me."

She showed us to our rooms and said we could come
and go as we pleased. "All six of my unfortunately de-
ceased husbands enjoyed their entertainment. So if you
feel the urge to partake of the pleasures afforded by
what's left of Six Points, I sincerely urge you to do so.
One or two right nice young women ply their trade at the

saloon and dance hall. And I hear the men who frequent the poker tables are generally most cordial."

We brought our possessions inside, excused ourselves, and headed back to town as fast as we could hoof it for whatever in the way of worldly distraction could be had. And on that particular night, the rapidly dying East Texas town of Six Points had plenty to offer.

Cutter hadn't been in the Lone Star Saloon two minutes when he headed upstairs with a cute little blond twitch named Trixie. Me and a hot-eyed, black-haired gal followed a few minutes later. But my choice for a little carnal pleasure turned out something of a bust after having been with fresh-as-peaches gals like Charlotte and Millie. Hell, that raven-topped Six Points girl looked right fine, but sweet glorious God, she had the worst breath I'd ever encountered from another living soul. Went to kiss her and almost passed out.

So, I did my business quick as I could, which is pretty fast when I put my mind to it, and headed back downstairs for the gambling, drinking, and other forms of manly entertainment. Found an open seat at a poker table surrounded by what appeared to be fairly pleasant company. In less than an hour, I'd turned the twenty dollars my partner staked me with into 280.

Course, I'll admit to consuming a bit more nose paint than I probably should have. Perhaps if I'd stayed upstairs with that nasty-mouthed gal, and not partaken of the questionable *espiritus fermenti* quite so heavily, an unpleasant episode later in the evening might never have occurred.

8

"You've been cheatin' like a son of a bitch."

My memory of the event has always been that I was about three hours into my cards, and cups, when it happened. Winning hands kept coming my way. Chips and cash had piled up to the tune of more than five hundred dollars. Felt pretty full of myself at the time. Dealer threw me a ten-high straight that trounced a poor goober holding a pair of aces.

The goober was a brute called Bruno. Bullet-headed thug worked the circus as a roustabout and, while he might have been some kind of genius at driving stakes in the ground and putting up tents, the man had no head for poker. Didn't keep him from having rather pointed opinions about my good fortune, though.

When the straight fell, he snarled, "You got a lot of money in front of you there, sonny boy. Sizable chunk of it's mine. Beginning to wonder just how you've managed to go and win so much."

Leaned back in the chair and eased a hand inside my coat to the pistol hanging in my shoulder rig. "Skill, my good fellow, skill. If you work at this game hard enough and pay attention, the mysterious intricacies of poker will eventually reveal themselves."

Most of the other gamblers must have had premonitions of my coming departure from this life, for they carefully scooted their chairs away and tiptoed to the nearest available corner.

"I think your run of luck has absolutely nothin' to do with knowledge of the game, skill, or anything resemblin' such blatherin' balderdash," Bruno growled.

Threw him a shocked smile and said, "What on earth are you implying, sir? Please tell me the exact nature of your distress. Spit it out. Perhaps I can do something to alleviate any misgivings you might harbor." I fear more than a little sarcasm might have crept into my voice at the time, but the big son of a bitch had begun to grate on my only remaining nerve.

Bruno twisted in a creaking chair. His ratty jacket fell open and revealed a Remington hand cannon behind the heavy leather belt cinched tightly around his thick waist. A ham-sized hand rested in his ample lap mere inches from the pistol's walnut grips. Under one of the fine dress coats I'd stolen from Elroy Cumby, I thumbed the hammer back on my short-barreled Colt and waited.

Angry bully snatched the well-chewed panatela from the corner of his yellow-stained lips, spit a sprig of tobacco across the table, and roared, "Well, if you must know, you thievin' little bastard, I'm a-thinkin' as how you've been cheatin' like a son of a bitch ever since setting down at the table with us traveling boys. My luck was runnin' pretty good till you plopped your narrow ass down."

God Almighty, but there just isn't anything can bring silence to a gambling establishment like use of the words "cheat," "cheating," or "cheater." Seems that everyone who frequents gaming tables has his ears pricked up and waiting for some ignorant jackass to make such an accusation so the real entertainment can start.

Got real quiet for at least ten feet in every direction around ole Bruno and me. Considerable number of attendees at that night's prayer meeting sucked away from our table and started making bets on which of us would survive his mean-mouthed accusation.

Out of the corner of my eye, I saw Cutter stroll up and take a spot near the bar, directly to my left. Felt pretty good, because I figured if Bruno the stake driver got lucky and killed me, he wouldn't live but about another second before Cutter turned him into a flour sifter.

"No cheating here. I'm simply better at the game and a lot luckier than anyone playing tonight. Tomorrow the cards could run in the exact opposite direction," I said. Had no intention of trying to stop the inevitable. Must admit, I was having fun.

Bruno gritted rotting teeth so hard, it sounded like buckets full of rocks rolling across the floor. "Nobody's that lucky, boy. I been playing poker all my adult life. Can spot a cheat sure as the man's head is painted red as a New England barn."

His stunningly foolish barn comparison was the one that sealed his fate for damned sure. I decided to kill him right then and there. But like a cat that can't stop playing with a dead mouse, I couldn't send him to Satan until after a little more fun at the thick-headed bastard's expense.

"Do hate to be the one to inform you of this, sir, but playing the game doesn't have a damned thing to do with whether you win or not."

He eyeballed me like I'd lost my mind. "Altogether, that's just about the stupidest goddamned thing I've ever heard come out of anyone's mouth."

"You didn't let me finish, Mr. Bruno, sir. As I was about to say, before being so rudely interrupted, winning requires a degree of talent and intelligence. You have displayed neither in this game. And the truth is, if I hadn't taken a seat, someone else would most likely have won all your money and be the object of your intemperate bile at this very moment."

A seriously perplexed look popped onto his broad, pockmarked face like someone had dropped a dead skunk on the table between us. "Are you callin' me stupid, you persnickety little twit? Takes a lotta goddamned nerve to call a man as dangerous as me stupid."

"Is that a fact?" I shot back. Then, out of nothing more than bald-faced recklessness, I delivered the spoken coup de grace. "Well, Bruno, bet I could keep you busy for a week searching for the top on a pistol ball. You're so righteously dumb, you'd have to study for ten or twelve years just to be a half-wit."

He went for his gun and, truth is, the big bastard got it out pretty quick. Unfortunately for him, the cavalry-model Colt he carried had about an inch too much barrel. It caught on the edge of the green felt playing surface. His first shot blasted a crater in the floor between my feet. Honest to God, looked like the table jumped six inches off the floor from the concussion of Bruno's horribly misguided aim. His eyes met mine as I thumbed off a round that hit him dead center. His shocked gaze dropped to the hole in his chest and he kicked his chair backward almost two feet.

Raw strength, and a dead man's determination, brought an arm as thick as a Tennessee plow horse's leg up for another try. His second blast sent a blue whistler burning harmlessly past my ear.

I stood, shifted the pistol to my weak side, and drew my hip gun. Ripped off four shots so fast they sounded like one thunderous explosion. A crimson spray of blood and bone squirted out Bruno's thick back, and his body jerked and flopped in the cane-backed chair each time one of my heavy slugs slapped into him.

Pandemonium went through the place with the vengeance of a West Texas cyclone. Men rushed about like chickens with their heads cut off. Liquor vendors ducked for cover behind their heavy oak bar. Women squealed, fell to the floor, and covered their heads with trembling hands. Overturned tables and chairs thudded and banged against one another as most of the panicked crowd jumped to their feet and headed for any available exit.

Holstered my pistols, snatched my hat off, and scraped all the money left on the table into it. As the dense black-powder smoke began to clear, Cutter eased up and stood by my side. He had a cocked pistol in each hand and over the noisy chaos around us yelled, "We've gotta get out of here as fast as we can, Eli. Them carnies find out you done went and killed one of theirs, and our lives will be about as worthless as tryin' to speak Chinese to a pig from Reynosa."

All the doors were jammed tight with people trying to get away from the shooting and dying. Cutter holstered one pistol, grabbed me by the arm, and hustled us toward the saloon's ornate front window on the far side of the room.

He fired his first shot at the top of the beveled pane less than ten feet away from the glass. His second round brought the whole thing down in a sparkling spray of jagged debris that crunched under our boots like gravel as we jumped through his newly made opening.

We'd tied our horses at the wrong end of the street, and were forced to run right through the middle of a raging knot of carnival folk who must have already learned of the kindly Mr. Bruno's unfortunate demise.

Cutter shouted, "News of a killin' does tend to travel fast in towns no bigger than this one. But, you know, the people who follow these damned carnivals seem to find out about such things like mind readers or something. Damned creepy if you ask me."

Luckily, a description of the man who'd sent Bruno the tent raiser to that great circus in the sky must not have made it to their angry red ears. I threw a hurried glance over my shoulder. Saw the carnival followers rage their way through the Lone Star's ruined window swinging ax handles, clubs, and barrel staves. Poor unfortunates who got in their way dropped like felled cottonwood trees.

"There's gonna be a lot of soreheaded folks around

here tomorrow morning," I said as we stepped into our
stirrups.

Cutter watched for less than five seconds before he
hissed, "Let's get the hell away from here, Eli. Bet it
won't take half an hour 'fore that snooty desk clerk at the
hotel gives me and you over to the mob. Blood-crazed
sons of bitches will be after us with a rope. You can bet
the ranch that if they catch us, we'll be the guests of honor
at an oak tree necktie party."

We kicked for Mrs. Scott's boardinghouse, stormed in,
and went to repacking all our belongings. Level of our
noisy entrance must have awakened her. She stumbled
into the hallway in her housecoat and said, "What on
earth's the problem, gentlemen?"

Cutter quickly explained our eventful evening in town,
and told her we'd best hit the trail as quickly as possible.
She expressed sincere regret that our brief stay with her
had to end, and said, "I'll pack you a meal to take along.
Have some leftover fried chicken and other things that
should be right tasty."

After leaving the kind lady three times her normal
room rate, we apologized for any problems our presence
might cause her in the future and fogged it west. Cutter
knew every back trail and hidden path in Texas. For the
next four days, we stayed as far out of sight as possible.

On our fifth day out, my partner said, "Well, ole son,
think we've spent enough time hidin' from the world.
Ain't been no detectable activity behind us. Might as well
get ourselves back to the high road and a bit in the way of
easier travelin'. Quicker we blend into the background of
Hell's Half Acre, the better."

A week later, we crossed the Texas and Pacific Railroad tracks south of Fort Worth near the depot and headed
up Main Street. Cutter said, "Let's stop at the first drinking establishment we come across. I'm mighty dry, Eli."

Reined up in front of a joint called the Local Option
Saloon. We were both pretty stiff from being in the saddle
for so long when we climbed off our animals and tied

them to the hitch. Had to stand in the dusty street and stretch for almost a minute before we could stumble to the boardwalk and the rustic establishment's batwing doors. Sign in the joint's front window advertised the rough-looking watering hole as having Fort Worth's "worst liquor, poorest cigars, and most miserable billiard tables."

Cutter eyeballed the Local Option's facade and said, "Maybe later we'll stroll over to the Palace. Lot bigger and nicer place than this 'un. Pay no attention to the sign. Feller who owns this place had some kind of disagreement with the city over liquor prohibition. He did that just to get attention. Musta worked, because you could barely get in here when the really big herds used to come through on their way to Kansas."

I'd only ever been to Fort Worth, or any other town of such size and renown, once before in my entire life. Pa had mostly kept his soul-saving business on a circuit in the rough hinterlands south of Austin. He justified this strange behavior by saying, "I don't have to confront the Devil in his own front yard to know that it's an iniquitous spot peopled by gamblers, drunkards, whores, whoremongers, pimps, and killers. My mission is to keep the fine folk of this pristine South Texas country from wanting to visit bilious blights like Fort Worth's tenderloin."

As a consequence, I'd spent most of my young life hoping and dreaming for an opportunity to fritter away as much time amongst the gamblers, drunkards, whores, whoremongers, pimps, and killers of Fort Worth as humanly possible. And now, a famed man killer I'd met by accident had led me into the most celebrated den of iniquity in all of Texas.

Only problem was that two things awaited me in Hell's Half Acre that I didn't expect and could easily have done without—fame and reputation. Both of them brought to my doorstep by an overly ambitious need to make some money and have a bit of fun.

9

"Do you want to die tonight, son?"

We stood at the Local Option's highly polished bar and had two drinks, and Cutter was ready to move on. "Lots to see and plenty to do," he said as we saddled up again and headed north on Main Street. "Have some special plans in mind for you, Eli. Gonna see, for certain sure, just how good you are with the pasteboards."

We'd almost reached the Emerald Saloon when I said, "What are you up to, Cutter?"

He threw me a sly grin. "Lots of gamblers pass through the Acre every day. They come here thinking to fleece any unsuspecting cowboy stupid enough to sit down at the table with them."

"Well, what makes you think I'd have any better chance against professionals than the trail hands?"

"You're gifted, boy. You can play and spy the cheat if one comes up better'n anyone I've ever seen. Might not know exactly how a cheater's doin' it, but I know you can spot it. Knowledge and skill beat cheatin' every time. Saw it back there in Six Points. Ain't a handful of folks can handle themselves at a poker table the way you do. See, gamblers don't make any money off each other. No, they're in it for the leather pounders, waddies, and shit kickers they can suck in and strip clean."

Decided there was nothing to be gained by telling Cutter about my gaming instructions at the knee of Diamond Jim back in Waco. Figured it might be interesting to go along with whatever he had in mind, and said, "Do I look like a real, honest-to-God brush popper?"

"Not yet. But you're gonna look like one. And you're gonna play like the slickest card bender who ever sat at a green felt table. It'll surprise 'em so bad, they won't know what hit 'em. I'll back you up. See to your safety. Be covering your back every second. All you have to do is play cards. Anybody gets testy like ole Bruno did, and I'll take care of 'em before the situation can get out of hand."

"What if I don't win?"

"Well, you might lose some. Most gamblers don't win all the time. But son, I've never seen anybody run 'em like you do. This is gonna be fun."

We rode past places like the Headlight Bar, Comique Saloon, Texas Wagon Yard, and a host of other equally attention-grabbing bars and sights. Cutter got us a room on the second floor of the El Paso Hotel. Had us a window that faced north. White Elephant Saloon and the Merchants Restaurant were right across the street. Country boy like me couldn't have been anymore impressed if he'd put us up in Pair-ree, France, at L'hôtel Grand.

Stretched myself out in a bed I could have died in when Cutter said, "You stay put for a bit, Eli. I'm gonna stable the horses. Do some shopping for you. Don't want anyone to see you till we've got your duds right. Won't be long, son. Don't be wandering around while I'm gone."

Took him about two hours before he got back. My empty stomach went to gnawing at my belt buckle, and I was just before heading across the street to the Merchants Restaurant when he stumbled into the room with an armload of clothing wrapped in brown butcher paper.

I busted one of the packages open and said, "Hell, Cutter, this stuff is used. Ain't nothing new here."

He held a faded bib-front shirt against my chest and said, "Of course it's used. Gotta make you look like an actual South Texas bronc-bustin' chuck-wagon follower who can ride anything with hair."

Cutter stood me in front of the mirror when he finished and said, "There you are. A lover, a fighter, and a wild bull rider. Bet there ain't one of these gamblin' sons of bitches will detect the fraud. We're gonna skin 'em six ways from Sunday, Eli." The faded shirt, rough canvas pants, run-down boots, Mexican spurs, and Boss of the Plains hat had me looking like a first-class wrangler, all right.

We had dinner in the hotel dining room. Took five hundred of the money I'd scooped off the table in Six Points and five hundred of Cutter's stash, and headed for the White Elephant. Guess it was around eight or nine o'clock by then. Joint was busier than a stomped-on anthill. People came and went in droves. We had to push our way into the front door.

Could have had a meal in the White Elephant's dining room, I suppose. Eating establishment was located on the first floor. Nicely appointed joint. Lots of dark paneling, heavy furniture, and etched glass everywhere. Gambling took place on the second floor, where you could play at tables in a common area near the bar, or in private rooms reserved mostly for the high rollers.

We sidled up to the bar, ordered a bottle, and I watched while Cutter gave the room and its occupants a careful eyeballing. Was pouring my second drink when he said, "No, Eli. One real tipple a night's all you get for as long as this dodge works. I'll see to it that the glass on your table is filled with nothing more than strong tea. It'll look enough like whiskey to fool anyone we set out to hoodwink."

Guess it might have sounded a bit testy when I

snapped, "I can hold my liquor. No need for anything so drastic as that."

"Trust me, boy. This is the best way. Want to keep your wits about you. Some of the men sitting in this room will kill you deader'n a rotten stump if they even suspect you might be the ringer at the table."

Resigned myself to the ruse and said, "Well, where do we start?"

He made a sweeping gesture across the room with the hand holding his glass. "See the table in the corner? Just a bunch of locals from the look of 'em. Can't detect any traveling sharpies. We'll start with them. Let 'em win two hundred or so, Eli. Then clean 'em out."

"How long you think we'll be here tonight?"

"Might be a spell. In fact, it'd be better if you take your time. Hell, all we've got is time on our hands. Lose big for a spell. Win big, lose a few. You can do it, son. We could walk out of here in the morning with thousands."

Sauntered over to the suckers he picked. Stood by their table watching till one of the players threw in his cards and vacated a chair. When I asked to sit in, five pairs of eyes lit up like the headlight on a Texas and Pacific freight. You could see it all over them. A defenseless waddie who'd arrived just in time to be skinned alive. Bastards planned to clean me out from the git-go. God Almighty, were they in for a surprise.

Ole Cutter's dodge was glorious. Whole deal worked exactly the way he'd planned. Them boys was one shocked bunch when I called it a night and walked off with damn near every cent they had to their names. When we stepped out onto the boardwalk early the next morning, I was wired up tighter than a banjo string. We counted out our winnings on the bed in our room. Total came to almost two thousand dollars.

Cutter said, "And that's from a bunch of low-life no-account locals. Nothing close to what passed over some of the tables around us." He spent till almost daylight trying to calm me down. I finally fell asleep about the time the sun came up. Just before noon, we had breakfast in the hotel dining room and made plans for our next raid.

"We'll lay out tonight, Eli. Just waltz over, have a few beakers of joy juice, and watch the action."

Cutter couldn't have picked a better word for that night's events. We'd been loafing at the bar for about two hours when an argument started at a table right in front of us.

Cowboy, dressed in a getup that could have passed him off as my brother, jumped to his feet and kicked his chair away. "That's it, you thievin' son of a bitch. Let it go by the board when I seen you going into your vest for the holdout card. Bein' as how you didn't win with it anyways. But by God, I'll not let you continue usin' that fancy diamond ring as a shiner to look at all the cards when you're dealin'." His hand rested on the butt of a silver-plated, stag-handled pistol, and, from all appearances, the slick-looking gent being dressed down was about to meet his Maker.

Local gambler I'd heard the bartender call Red Connor pushed his silk top hat to the back of his head and placed both hands on the table. Feller was decked out as cocky as the king of spades. Real peaceful, he said, "You need to calm down. Seems you think I'm trying to cheat you, friend. Let me assure you, this game is square. Nothing underhanded here."

"Now you done went and compounded your sin, card-sharp. Lyin' ain't quite as bad as cheatin', but it's damned close. You might think me stupid, mister, but I've been around the bush a time or two and know when the brace is on. If this game is square, I rode in sidesaddle this afternoon on a sow."

Bartender leaned over between me and Cutter and yelled, "Take it outside, gents. You know better, Red. You're disturbing our other players. Management don't want no trouble in here. Keep it up, and I'll call the marshal."

Feller in the silk hat said, "No trouble, Mr. Jackson. My overly anxious opponent is just about to leave before something awful happens."

Cowboy snorted, "Is that a fact? And just what son of a bitch is gonna make me?"

Red raised his right arm about six inches off the table. I heard something that sounded like metal snapping, and, as if by magic, a four-barreled derringer appeared in his hand.

Disgruntled cowhand flinched and, real calm, the gentleman sharpie said, "Do you want to die tonight, son?" His other hand came up and a matching pistol appeared in it. Poor waddie was staring down eight barrels of primed, cocked, and ready potential death.

I was dumbfounded. Like a kid who'd just seen a traveling magician make doves appear out of a flaming tambourine. How those tiny poppers materialized was a total mystery to me at the time.

Cutter chuckled. He whispered, "Think our hot-mouthed buckaroo best give up on this argument or get hisself killed deader'n a rusted brandin' iron."

Guess the dissatisfied cow chaser came to the same conclusion. His hand drew away from the fancy-gripped Colt, and he headed for the stairs. But on the first step, he turned and said, "This ain't over, not by a damned sight. You are an irritant and a vexation to me of the first water, and we'll take this up again at another time."

Red Connor snapped, "Keep walking or suffer the consequences."

Threat didn't scare the fast-talking wrangler. He said, "While you deal in cards, you pasteboard-bendin' son of a bitch, I deal in lead. Best watch your back, tinhorn." Then he scurried away like a lizard looking for a nice cool rock to hide under.

Cutter fired up a cigarette and placed his hand on my shoulder. "Take this as a free lesson, Eli. There's more'n a good chance that most of these professional types cheat at one time or another. But if you're gonna accuse one of them of not being on the up and up, always draw first, and then hit 'em with your claim. Don't ever give one of these bastards an inch. If you do, he'll take a mile, and you might end up dead, or put to shame like that poor stupid goober who just flounced out of here."

"Damn, Cutter, think I'd like to have me a set of whatever that gambler's got up his sleeve that causes those little pistols to pop out like they did."

"Cumbersome rod-and-spring contraption that straps to your arm. You're better off with that fine Colt of yours holstered across your belly. Lot more powerful and intimidating. Just as easy to draw and fire."

While we'd planned to lay out that night, the easily available, recently vacated seat at the sharpie's table was just too good to pass up. I sat in on the game and spent most of the evening trying to figure out if the irate cowboy might have been accurate. Never was able to detect anything amiss. And best of all, came away a winner when the game finally broke up at about two the next morning.

Cutter and I took our leave of the Elephant a step or so ahead of the other men at the table. We'd barely passed through the front entrance when I spotted the still-fuming leather pounder. He skulked in a badly lit alleyway across Main between the Centennial Theatre and Merchants Restaurant.

"Guess who I just spotted, Cutter."

"I seen him 'fore we got to the boardwalk," my friend said. "Let's get the hell out of the way, Eli. Don't want the law lookin' to me for testimony on this one. We'll watch, and then get the hell out of here soon as the shootin's over."

"You really believe they'll shoot it out?"

"Not one doubt in my mind," he said, and pulled me to a spot on the south wall closest to our hotel.

Red Connor strolled into the street and appeared totally oblivious to what awaited him. Man couldn't have taken more than half a dozen steps when I heard his outraged adversary yell, "You owe me money, you card-cheatin' son of a bitch."

Well, that got ole Red's attention for sure. He stopped dead in his tracks, slowly removed a cigarette from his lips, and searched the darkness for the origin of the threat.

Leaned Cutter's direction and whispered, "Think the gambler might be a bit shortsighted. Doesn't appear he's able to see very far in the dark."

'Bout then, the cowboy stomped from his alleyway hidey-hole and into the street. Looked to me as though the adversaries were probably a good fifty or sixty feet apart at the time.

"You've got three hundred of mine in your poke, card-sharp. Worked hard for that money. Pushed critters more'n five year in order to save up for the future. Ain't about to leave town without it."

"You lost every penny of that money to me fair and square," Red said.

"Damned if I did," the wrangler yelled.

"Damned if you didn't," Red yelled back.

"Hand over the three hundred or die where you stand, you low-life thievin' bastard."

Cutter whispered, "Well, it don't get much plainer than that. Red can't get out of this one. He's either gonna have to throw down the cash, and thereby admit he's a card cheat, or fight."

I said, "Won't be much of a contest at that distance. Take a hell of a shot to hit the Merchants Restaurant with those tiny pistols Red's carrying."

Guess I'd barely got out the last word when the gambler's arms came up. Fire shot a foot from the barrels of both his pistols, but he couldn't have hit his challenger's horse at that distance. Derringers made popping noises like someone breaking empty bottles against a board fence. Doubt he even woke anyone up. Disturbance Red caused didn't amount to any more than kids shooting off wet firecrackers.

Nervy brush popper didn't so much as flinch. Leisurely drew his pistol, turned sideways like an old-timer fighting a formal duel over a lady's chastity, took careful aim, and pulled the trigger on his long-barreled cavalry-model Colt. Thunderous muzzle blast shattered the night.

Heavy slug slapped into Red Connor's chest and shoved him backward two or three steps. One hand darted to the wound as he fired a shot into the ground with the other. Unused pistol uselessly dangled from the steel-rod contraption attached to his arm, and got in the way of the hand grabbing at the blood-squirting hole in his vest.

Wounded man swayed for two or three seconds before a second shot tore through the air, ripped into his body, and knocked him to his knees. Looked as though he was trying to lift an anvil when a limp arm came about halfway up and fired another harmless popper at nothing in particular. Then he rolled onto his side, kicked at the air like a dying horse, and finally stopped moving.

The cowboy strolled over to the twice-shot gambler as unhurried as a man on the way to a Baptist church social. He stopped a step from the bleeding heap at his feet and toed the body. Man was mighty surprised when the gambler rolled over and fired two shots right into his crotch. Pistol couldn't have been more than an inch away from the shocked buckaroo's canvas pants when it went off. Burning powder from the muzzle set the material on fire.

Damnation, but the wound must have hurt something monstrous. Silly son of a bitch screamed like a cat what got its tail caught under Grandma's rocker. Big pistol flew out of his hand like he had hold of a molten horseshoe. He grabbed his privates, went to slapping at the flames, hopped around the street, fell down, rolled in all the filth and horse manure, and yelped for so long, I thought about putting him out of his misery myself.

Cutter leaned against the wall and laughed like a crazy man. Shook his head and said, "That's gotta be the damnedest gunfight I've ever seen."

Took my hat off and slapped my leg with it. "Haven't

seen that many myself. Sure wouldn't want to get shot in the *huevos* like that, though."

People poured out of the saloons and gambling houses along both sides of the street. Feller who claimed to be a doctor rushed up, examined Red Connor, and announced that he'd passed. Poor bastard with the flaming crotch was still hollering to beat the band when they toted him away. Cutter and me headed for our room as fast as we could hoof it.

Next morning at breakfast, we heard that ole Red's aim couldn't have been any better if he'd planned the whole event. Overheard a whiskey drummer at the table next ours say, "Yessir, blew both of 'em off, clean as a whistle. Hear tell the doctor said as how he couldn't have taken 'em off any cleaner with a sharp knife and an hour to do the cuttin'. Damnedest thing I've ever witnessed."

Feller at the same table nursed his coffee and said, "You observed the gunplay?"

"That I did, sir," the drummer bragged. "Had just exited the El Paso Saloon, one of my best customers, when the shoutin' and shootin' started. Hell of a gunfight. One I'm not likely to forget. First time I've ever seen a man set ablaze by pistol fire."

Cutter leaned across our table and said, "You see that blowhard on the street last night, Eli?"

"Not that I remember."

"Me neither. Amazin', ain't it. Some folks just can't pass up an opportunity for the least bit in the way of attention. They'll lie like dogs as long as there's an audience that's willing to listen."

Next day, Red Connor's grieving wife had him buried in Fort Worth's Oakwood Cemetery. Can't imagine why my friend did it, but Cutter insisted we attend.

Methodist preacher conducted the services. He did a right fine job, too. Afterward, Cutter and I lingered by the grave for a bit. His reaction to the whole turn of events surprised me.

Got right misty-eyed when he twisted at the brim of his

hat and said, "Killed more'n my share, Eli. Figure God is gonna make me pay up for those sins pretty soon."

Put a hand on his shoulder and said, "Aw, hell, Cutter, no need to get sentimental on me."

"This kind of thing doesn't usually have much effect on me, but the day Connor got shot was my birthday. Turned fifty years old while we watched him bite the dust. I'm ancient for a gunfighter. Feel like my time's comin' soon."

Jesus, I had no idea what to say. Didn't appear to be any way to comfort him. Over the short time we'd been together, felt I'd grown closer to the man than the Reverend and I'd ever been. So I simply let it drop, and once we got away from the graveyard, he perked right up. But, hell, sometimes a man sees death coming when no one else does. Leastways, I know Cutter did.

10

"You shot a state senator eight times . . . ?"

For over a month, Cutter and I lived like kings. Second week into our Fort Worth raid, we started a circuit of the Acre's most popular gambling joints. My partner allowed as how the plan would keep our faces from becoming too familiar at any given site. His idea must have worked, because we accumulated an astonishing amount of money, and no one seemed any the wiser as to what we were doing.

Got to the point where I looked forward to playing in certain locations. Came to genuinely enjoy the companionship offered by Henry Burns's Club Room, R.J. Winder's Cattle Exchange Saloon, and smaller joints like the Tivoli and Occidental. But the Elephant remained my favorite, and I was always at my best on the nights we played there.

Everything proceeded along swimmingly, couldn't have been any better. And then one night, the entire bottom of our galvanized washtub fell through when Cutter accidentally bumped into a grubby stack of walking dung on the boardwalk in front of the Theatre Comique. We'd had a few too many of the Bismark's "cold as ice itself" beers and were on our way back to our room at the time. Pair of rude sons of bitches stumbled from an alleyway and almost knocked both of us onto our backs.

Cutter cussed the bastards in a stream of blue language that would have shamed the devil. But afterward, I noticed something must have occurred during the encounter that weighed mighty heavy on his mind. Got to where he spent an uncommon amount of time looking over his shoulder, and when I gambled, he backed into a corner rather than sitting in a chair near my table.

Several nights of his strange behavior finally got the best of me. On the way to the Elephant for what I expected to be another profitable evening, I placed my arm around his shoulders and said, "What's on your mind, Cutter?"

"Oh, I've just been a bit anxious the past few days," he said.

"What's to be anxious about? We're doing great."

"Remember those two drunks we bumped into the other night?"

Thought it very odd he would bring up the subject of two insignificant inebriates that meant nothing to me. "Of course I remember. You cussed the hell out of 'em."

"Sure did. Well, the one who shouldered me looked familiar. Been tryin' to place him ever since. Bad part is he keeps showing up in odd places. Always watchin' us. Has a sneaky aspect to him. His idiot-looking partner is even less cautious in the way he eyeballs where we go and what we're doin'. I think they're following us, Eli."

"You sure? Could be they're just a pair of whiskey-chasing sots who frequent the same places we do."

"I suppose. But I've seen 'em both somewheres before. Haven't been able to place the bastards yet, but I will."

Thought that was the end of the discussion. Leastways, I hoped so. But midway through that very evening's play, felt a tug at my sleeve and Cutter was pointing at the bar. Sure enough, both strangers stood at the far end of the Elephant's highly polished counter, sipped on double shots of scamper juice, and worked much harder than necessary to look as though not interested in what we were doing.

My friend appeared some agitated, so I excused myself from the game, and we moved to an empty table. He leaned over and whispered, "Recognize him now, Eli. Finally came to me when I saw them stroll up the stairs tonight like they was just here for a friendly drink. One with the handlebar mustache is none other than Mathias Slate. Big bastard sportin' the cauliflower nose, backin' him, is Jonas Wakefield. Never seen one without the other bein' close by."

He'd left me lying in the dirt. I didn't recognize either name. Hell, there was really no reason why a hen wrangler like me should have been acquainted with such men. Said, "Know you think I've been around almost as much and as long as you, Cutter, but I have no idea who they are. Want to enlighten me?"

"Mathias Slate is a bounty hunter. Usually works an area from San Antonio south. He and Jonas can boast of being very successful. If a man's been posted and there's money to be made, they'll be after him sooner or later."

Subtle urgency in his voice brought me to ask, "Think these men are here for you?"

Cutter didn't miss a beat when he said, "Very likely. Hell, they's posters on me hanging from damn near every tree down that way, 'specially around Gonzales. Even if Slate's not here for a reward, he's been known to hire his gun out for those who wish to buy a bit of cheap revenge."

"That scruffy son of a bitch is a killer for hire?"

He rolled a smoke, and lit up before saying, "Yep, and a damned good one. Hear tell he's killed upward of thirty men. Bests me by at least ten."

"What the hell did you do in Gonzales that would send someone out looking for a hired gun?"

Several smoke rings made it to the Elephant's tin ceiling before he replied. "Had a run-in with a state senator down that way. Arrogant son of a bitch was causin' more'n a bit of trouble for a lady friend of mine. Caught him on the road to Seguin one afternoon and told him how the cow ate the cabbage. Stupid jackass went to reachin' and grabbin' for his pistol. Wasn't what anyone would call a very smart move on his part. Had to shoot him."

Don't know why, but I asked, "How many times?"

"Eight."

Struck me as some funny. Snorted out a giggle and said, "You shot a state senator eight times because of a woman? This the same man Spook McCain braced us over?"

He thumped ashes into the spittoon. "Yeah, the very one. Figured I might as well make sure he was dead. Ain't no profit in shootin' anyone, 'less you make damned sure they won't come back and get you. Besides, she was a damned fine woman. Worth killin' a state senator for. Thing I forgot is that rich bastards always have family."

As one day passed to another, I got to thinking that maybe Cutter had made a mistake. Didn't have any effect on how he acted, though. Kept on looking over his shoulder, and one night I noticed as how he'd moved us to the middle of the street rather than using the boardwalks. Then, on the fourth or fifth night after he pointed Slate and Wakefield out in the Elephant, the sons of bitches braced us.

We'd rogued our way from the better part of town, down to the Emerald Saloon for a relaxing evening of unfettered drinking, and were on our way back to the hotel. Got to the corner of Sixth and Main Streets. Strolled along a dimly lit area near the board fence on the west side of the Texas Wagon Yard. Cutter had sprung for an evening cigar fresh from Cuba. We were luxuriating in deep tobacco heaven when both them evil sons of bitches jumped out in front of us less than twenty feet away.

Mathias Slate held a hand up and yelped, "That's far enough, Cutter."

My friend didn't waste a second responding. "I knew you'd get around to whatever evil brought you to me, Slate."

Jonas Wakefield stood slightly behind and to the left of his butt-ugly partner. Probably isn't exactly true, but I thought I could smell the filthy son of a bitch. He scratched, hocked up a gob of something awful, spit my direction, and shifted from foot to foot. Every five seconds or so, his right hand would make a slight move toward the grip of an old Colt's Dragoon, and then dart back to the massive Mexican silver buckle holding his belt up.

I whispered, "Don't worry about Wakefield, Cutter. I'll take him if he makes the wrong move."

Slate stood spraddle-legged with his thumbs hooked over his pistol belt. "Senator Hightower's family wants you back in Gonzales. They figure to put you on trial for the foul and unnatural murder of a devoted family man and well-known Texas legislator. And after a suitable verdict of guilty as hell, by God, they figure on hangin' the shit out of your sorry ass."

His smart-mouthed arrogance really got my goat. I snapped, "Sounds like you expect a fine afternoon of entertainment from the Hightower family's murderous plans."

For the first time, Wakefield chimed in. He shook a finger my direction and said, "We'ens ain't got no truck with you, boy. Time fer you to step aside. Don't want to go answerin' to local lawdogs fer shootin' no innocent citizen."

Cutter let a nervous chuckle escape. "How come you didn't handle this situation the way you usually do, Mathias?"

Slate scratched his chin. "And what way would that be, Sharpe?"

Cutter sneered and said, "Oh, from what I hear, your normal routine usually involves stepping from an alley and shootin' your intended victim in the back. Ain't that right?"

Slate smiled so big that even in the poor light I could see his tobacco-stained teeth. "Now that's a terrible thing to say, Cutter. Terrible, but true. As it happens, Beauregard Hightower, son of the previously mentioned senator, wants you alive. He's determined to see your neck stretched. Personally told me as how he's gonna giggle like a schoolgirl when you mess your drawers."

Cutter growled, "Ain't neither one of you back-shootin' dogs good enough to take me head-on, Slate. You're gonna have to resort to past practices. Even you aren't stupid enough to think I'd just give up my pistol and go to my own hanging. Now, either go for your gun, or get the hell out of my way."

Must have been about five seconds worth of indecision before that idiot Wakefield forced the situation. His hand darted for the almost worthless piece of iron in his belt. Barrel of the Dragoon never cleared for action. Used all the speed, and every trick Cutter had ever taught me, when I whipped out both Elroy Cumby's beautiful Peace-makers.

As there were no buildings within a block in any direction of where we stood, the ripping crack from the shots I thumbed off thundered away in every direction, and swirled around us in a watery wall of noise. Wakefield staggered backward as four massive slugs driven by thirty-eight grains of black powder slammed into his chest.

Silly bastard staggered two or three steps, glanced down at the holes in his chest, and said, "Merciful Father. Little son of a bitch done went and kilt me, Mathias."

The speed and accuracy of my response stunned Mathias Slate into a split second's worth of hesitation. A single eyeblink of time was all Cutter needed.

The instant Slate realized death had ten bony fingers wrapped around his worthless neck, Cutter drew and fired a red-hot slug that punched a hole between the bounty man's eyes that could have passed for something accomplished with a sharpened drill bit.

Gout of blood and bone the size of my fist flew from the back of his skull. Traveled about a foot, and turned into a cloud of spraying gore. Odd thing, though. While Wakefield dropped like an anvil in a rain barrel when he went down, Mathias swayed as you might imagine a weeping willow would in a stiff breeze. Pistol slipped from dead fingers as he turned, stumbled three or four steps, and fell on his face.

Cutter grabbed me by the sleeve and hissed, "Holster your pistols and follow me, Eli."

He dragged me west to Houston Street. As we turned north toward the hotel, he said, "Slow down. Take your time. Walk like nothing is amiss. Law's gonna be looking for someone running away from the scene. If we meet anybody, tell 'em you saw two men hoof'n it toward the Texas and Pacific Depot."

Sure enough, we'd barely gone half a block when a couple of fellers waving pistols and wearing deputy marshal's badges came running our direction. Brawny brute who looked like you could bounce cannonballs off his head stopped and growled, "Hold it right there, boys."

Cutter pulled up, threw his hands in the air, and said, "Thank God, Officer. You're just the men we wanted to find. Couple of fellers got into a pistol fight with two or three other men over yonder by the wagon yard. Shootin' started, and we got away from there as quick as possible."

The bruiser's miniature partner squeaked, "You seen what happened?"

Sounded like a scared Sunday School teacher when I said, "Yes, sir, we did. And we also seen which way the murderin' skunks what kilt them poor boys a-layin' in the street went whence they runned away from their highenous crimes. They's a-headed for the railroad depot. If'n you start now, might just be able to catch 'em afore they gits lost amongst all them cars down in the freight yard."

Pocket-watch-sized deputy yelped, "Come on, Brutus. If'n we catch us a couple of killers, marshal will love us till we die."

Took about two seconds for those poor dumb-assed boys to forget we even existed and burn boot leather for the Texas & Pacific station. We kept up our leisurely pace and headed directly to the hotel.

Cutter threw open the door to our room, snatched his hat off, wiped a sweat-drenched brow, and said, "Whew. Was a close 'un, Eli." He dropped the hat in a chair and flopped onto his bed.

"Aw, hell, Cutter, wasn't that close. Those poor stupid goobers simply fell for a great ruse. Glad you thought of it."

"Yeah, well, no matter how you slice it, that big son of a bitch had us in his sights, and things could have gone either way but for the runt. Hadn't been for your amazin' imitation of a pumpkin-rollin' plow-pusher, we'd probably be sittin' in a cell down at the city jail this very minute."

"Learned how to talk like that from traveling with my father. We had Sunday dinner with so many farmers, I sometimes thought I'd wake up one morning and discover God had turned me into a country-fried chicken."

Cutter let loose with a strangled laugh, and then fell silent for near five minutes. Finally, he threw me a pained look and said, "We're gonna have to split up. Get the hell out of Fort Worth as quick as we can, son. Tomorrow morning won't be too soon."

Surprised the hell out of me. Couldn't understand why he'd come to such a conclusion. "What for?" I asked. "No need to worry about them two deputies. Them boys couldn't identify us if we were the only two men left in town who could possibly have dropped a hammer on Slate and Wakefield."

My trail mate, and close friend, had a pained look on his face when he said, "Don't matter, Eli. Look, son, I've taught you all I can about guns. Think you're probably better'n me with a pistol now. We've done well with the gambling. Figure we'll each get about five thousand in the split. Don't fool yourself. Hell's Half Acre might appear totally lawless, but they've got a marshal here who'll find out what happened down by the wagon yard tonight. You can bet everything we've got on it."

"That's damned hard to believe. We were the only people there. No one else saw what happened."

"Don't believe that one for a second. Anytime some empty-headed son of a bitch gets his sad self killed, you can bet someone else saw it. By tomorrow noon, the law's gonna be pounding on that door over yonder with a warrant for our arrests. I know it's hard to take, but we've got to split up, get away from here tonight."

Took less than an hour to pack our belongings, pay our hotel and stable bills, and hit the road running. We headed in a kind of westerly direction—out toward Mineral Wells. Didn't quit running till about noon the next day.

Guess we'd gone about twenty miles when Cutter reined up on a scrubby hill. He said, "Here's where we part, Eli. I'm gonna turn north. Head for the Indian Nations. Once I get across the Red River, it won't matter who they send after me. Man can get lost in the Nations— without even trying much."

Whole turn of events still had my head spinning. Actually didn't believe he'd really split us up. But he looked more troubled than I could remember. From the way he acted, my good friend was in a hurry to move on.

"Think I'll mosey down toward Gonzales," I said. "My pa used to preach to some right nice folk down that way. Ranchers mainly. Might see if I can hire on with one of them. Lay low for a spell. Try to keep out of trouble. Never worked cattle. Might be fun."

Cutter turned away and gazed north. "Sounds like a

good plan. I'd stay away from any of those places where you left bodies in your wake. They's posters out on you by now. Especially around La Honda. And whatever you do, don't go back to Nacogdoches. Killin' a lawman, even one as worthless as Clinton Turnbow, ain't gonna be forgot anytime soon."

"Never thought of living this way, Cutter. Suppose I'd best avoid Waco, too."

"You live by the gun now, Eli. Every town you've put a man in the ground is a place you'd best avoid."

"Don't sound like much of a life, amigo. Never thought about how I'd live the rest of my days when I killed those men."

"You're right, Eli. It ain't much of a life. Our brief stay in Fort Worth was the best time I've had in more'n five years. Hell, the Acre was about the only place left where I could walk the streets and not be recognized. That's why I'm headin' for the Nations."

He offered his hand. I shook it, and we parted as good friends. Just before he rode away, Cutter said, "Gonna be hard to stay alive from now on, son. Whatever comes your way, don't hesitate to protect yourself. Real easy to get dead out in the wild places. Keep 'em primed, Eli. Hope we meet again."

But I never saw him again. Came to the belief that sometimes hope's not worth a bucket of spit. Sure as hell wasn't as far as me and Cutter were concerned.

Some months later, I heard he'd been killed in a fight with a posse of Hangin' Judge Parker's deputy marshals. Way the story went, they caught him stealing horses up around McAlester. Never believed it for a second. Wasn't Cutter's style. Whole time we rode together, the man never so much as breathed anything about stealing livestock. Personally, I think he's still alive and living up on the Canadian River somewhere. Holed up in a nice little cabin with a beautiful Indian maiden.

Pointed myself southeast. Lived the way he'd taught me. Stayed away from the larger towns. Only went into one-horse, one-drink burgs when I needed supplies. But after about three weeks of running and hiding like a wild animal, I craved poker, female company, and something to drink. Stopped in Mexia. Damnation, but that was a bloody mistake.

11

"I'll kill you where you stand."

As the end of my life rapidly approaches, I've given the events that led me into murderous habits some considerable thought. Have come to the undeniable conclusion that nothing short of heavenly intervention could have stayed me from my appointment with destiny. Certainly not the incident in Mexia.

Yessir, if I had to suggest a single episode in the blood-drenched years between my birth and where I find myself now as an object lesson in how *not* to live out your days, Mexia might well be the worst of it. Hell, I'm pretty damned certain missionaries could use my Mexia tale as an example of how to scare kids back into the arms of the Lord.

The tiny settlement was no more than a wide spot in a dirt road when I arrived—kind of community most Texans would refer to as a Saturday afternoon town. Refers to one where folks gather on Saturday, but where there isn't much going on any other time of the week. A place so small, you could miss it even if you didn't blink. Looked like an outstanding spot to lay low at the time.

A bank, general mercantile, barbershop, livery, six-room hotel, café, four saloons, telegraph office, damn near nonexistent jail, and a church comprised the entire, whole, and complete hamlet. Total population couldn't have amounted to more than two or three hundred on the busiest market day of the year. Best of all, the nearest law was almost forty miles away in Waco.

I took the best room available at the Metropolitan Hotel. In spite of its impressive name, that's not saying a whole bunch. But it served a single traveler like me well enough. Discovered in pretty short order, from an overly friendly desk clerk named Tobias Greeb, that a nonstop poker game in the Palace Saloon drew semiskilled card benders and some fairly good money for the patient player.

Being as how I didn't have anywhere special to go, and had plenty of cash in my pockets, figured I could sleep till noon, have lunch across Front Street at the Crescent Café, play poker for a year, and still have change left even if I lost at every hand. And if the cards fell the way I actually expected, my stash of ready money would grow into an even larger pile for future use.

Morning after arriving, I strolled two doors down Front Street to the Palace for a gander. An elegant entrance was the grandest thing about the joint. Set of beautifully fashioned mahogany batwing doors greeted thirsty visitors.

Like many cow-country saloons, the Palace sported a fine-looking bar on the right side of a long narrow room. Tables and chairs sat on a rough-cut board floor and lined the left, no more than three or four steps away from easy access to the liquor. Sign over a separate area at the back of the room indicated it had once been reserved for dancing, but from all appearances, any available women had vamoosed for more rewarding climes. High ceiling and fans cranked by a Mexican, sitting in a corner, offered visitors a nice respite from the outside heat. All around the room, polished spittoons awaited the day's customers.

Substantial-looking gent behind the bar wore green garters on his arms and had a head like an oiled cue ball. He glanced up when I entered, smiled, and said, "Morning, stranger. Come right in. The Palace is a bit cooler than the street."

"Nice place you've got here," I said, and slid up to the bar. "Cool, peaceful, solid, like you've been here a spell."

Bartender smiled. A gold front tooth twinkled as he said, "At the Palace, we like to think of ourselves as small but comfortable, sir. Great place to pass the time, play poker, have a cold beer, or simply visit with friends."

"Along with all your other good points, cold beer is a mighty fine recommendation, sir."

"No formality here. Everyone calls me Red. Red Parker." He flashed his sparkling tooth again and added, "Holdover from those bygone days of departed hair."

"Bet it was a sight to behold," I said.

"Came down to my shoulders and curled like a baby's. Women loved it."

I raised my hands as if giving up on a fight. "Believe every word, friend. What about one of your *cold* beers?"

"Was just before telling you all about that. Had a ten-foot-deep cellar dug out back when refrigeration arrived in Waco. Line it with fifty-pound blocks of ice, brought in by wagon twice a week. No brag or bluster to say I've got the frostiest beer in these parts. Ain't another establishment in town can declare as much."

He toweled off a spot on the bar in front of me, drew a chilly mug of golden goodness, winked, and said, "Enjoy."

Figured there was no reason to use my real name, so I offered my hand and said, "Henry Moon, Red. Here to indulge my weakness for a little poker. Should events work out the way I hope, might even settle in for an extended visit." We shook and were good friends from then on.

He pointed to a table in the far corner, next to the former dance hall entrance. "Best spot is yonder, Mr. Moon. Take your beer and have a seat. I'll bring over a bowl of roasted peanuts. Players usually start drifting in around ten. Think you'll find the society at the Palace most cordial."

By the end of that first week, Red Parker's prediction had proven absolutely accurate. Men from every imaginable walk of life gathered by early afternoon for an agreeable round of cards, friendly association, and a taste of John Barleycorn. Cowhands, a banker, a telegrapher, clerks, and farmers appeared at one time or another. They came and went as singles and in pairs. Some played all afternoon and into the night. Some could only sit in for a few hours. Many flopped into their chairs covered with a heavy layer of dust from a day's hard work, while others were scrubbed pink and smelled of fragrant toilet waters.

Had been at my chosen profession but a few days when several of the regular players invited me to visit their church for Sunday services. On an impulse, I decided to attend. My return to the bosom of the Lord proved more inspirational than I could have imagined. A number of the congregation's lovely young women added considerably to my sincere feelings of being uplifted. They usually lifted me up during secret visits to my room, between midnight and four in the morning. There were times during some of those passionate dances when I would have sworn I saw God.

The experience of being back in the familiar territory of Christian fellowship proved so elevating, I felt a new outfit was in order. Cutter's cowboy duds had grown a bit out of place for my purposes. Decided a churchgoing gambler should dress the part. Visited Harlan's Mercantile the next day, and purchased two stylish-looking black suits, six new white shirts, a red-blue-and-black tie, and a Sunday-go-to-meeting hat. Usually sat on the front pew, and within a month, almost everyone in town called me Deacon Moon.

The days passed most pleasantly for more than six months. Before I realized what had occurred, my routine had become so congenial that the lethal and blood-splattered turmoil of the past faded to a seldom-visited spot in my quickly healing memory.

Every morning, I usually ate a hearty breakfast at Carlotta Roberts's Crescent Café. Jolly, and stout from sampling her own cooking, the lady greeted all my visits as though she'd found a long-lost son. By noon, I'd taken up my favorite spot at the Palace, and on Sundays, the Reverend Silas Castleberry hit me with a healthy dose of hellfire and brimstone.

Suppose the best word to describe my situation would be contented. Eli Gault was contented for the first time in his chaotic life. But, as old-timers like to remind us, just when you think life can't get any better, God has a habit of setting your head to ringing like a tenpenny nail hit with a ball-peen hammer.

Happened one lightning-spiked night when a change for the worse blew through the Palace's front door in the form of four slicker-draped, soaking-wet strangers. Discovered later the leader of the bunch's name was Hector Pine and, of the three friends who accompanied him, it would have been difficult to determine which man could boast of the most belligerent disposition.

Soon as the angry-browed quartet bellied up to the bar, Pine bellowed, "Bring me and my friends a drink, you lazy bastard, and be damned quick about it."

More than friendly enough from my viewpoint, Red said, "No need to shout. My pleasure to serve you, sir."

Stranger wrestled a cavalry-model Colt from under his rain garb and laid the seven-and-a-half-inch barrel across Red's bulbous nose. Everyone at the table with me heard the bone crack all the way across the room. Blood spurted from a nasty cut left by the pistol's ejector rod as Red's eyes flipped into the back of his head. He leaned against the sturdy back bar, grabbed a bar rag from his waistband, and clamped it over the gushing wound.

Cliff Stoops, a fearless ranch hand who sat beside me, said, "No need for such behavior in here, you son of a bitch. You want to show your ass, take it across the street to the Red Light. Drunken scum over there like your type."

When the leader of the group turned from the bar, the others came around with him like mechanical figures on the front of a cuckoo clock. One-eyed feller closest to our table cocked his head to the side and growled, "Best keep that lip of yer'n buttoned, you shit-kicking bastard. Otherwise, Grizz here might take offense." He placed a hand on the arm of the monster to his left, who giggled like something dangerous and insane.

Red tried to smooth the situation over. He ran around the bar, held up a calming hand, and through the blood-soaked towel still held tightly to his nose, snuffled, "Gentlemen, gentlemen. No harm done. It was my fault. Didn't mean to sound uppity, sir. Don't want no trouble in the Palace. Please accept my most humble apology."

Weasely-looking ruffian at the opposite end of the bar from where Mr. One Eye stood said, "You cornpone-eatin' chicken wranglers obviously don't know who you're dealin' with. My name's Manfred Crouch."

Got the impression he expected us all to know him and fear his reputation. Sounded right belligerent to me. When no one responded, Crouch hooked a thumb at his leader. "This here's Hector Pine. Feller on his right's Grizz Jacks. And my friend with the patch is One-Eyed Frank Troy. Sure you've all heard of us. We're a right bad bunch, loaded for bear and lookin' for trouble."

No doubt about it, they damned sure were. I could tell by the glint in their blank, dead eyes the Pine bunch wanted to kill somebody. And it didn't really matter who.

The Palace got real quiet. All of a sudden, no one from Mexia wanted to add anything to the conversation. Not sure exactly what came over me. Started at my toes and burned a hot path all the way to the sweatband in my hat. Those bastards had been in my presence less than five minutes and I'd heard everything I ever wanted from them from that moment until the Rapture. Besides, they'd interrupted my game, destroyed the fellowship I'd grown to value, spoiled for a fight, and on top of everything else, guess I'd been a well-behaved Christian feller for way too long. Something hot and deadly flared in my guts.

Carefully checked to make sure all my pistols rested in the right places and were easily reached. Hip gun, belly piece, and backup felt loose and ready to deal death and destruction when called upon.

Slipped icy fingers around the grips of my crossover gun, pushed my hat to the back of a cold, sweat-drenched head, and said, "Do believe it best for you gentlemen to take your business elsewhere. Whatever tale you've got to tell, you can do it walking."

Soon as I finished, everyone at my table stood and moved to spots they considered safer. The weasel snapped to attention like he'd been slapped by a ten-year-old girl. "Didn't you hear me? Thought I done warned you that we're dangerous men."

Stood and pulled my suit coat back. Dressed in black from head to foot, have to admit I must have appeared quite a dangerous-looking figure. My bone-handled pistols damn near glowed in the lamplight. Hell, the way I figured it, those idiots would have a helluva tough time getting weapons from under their rain slickers. It's one thing to buffalo a bartender when you've got plenty of time to do it. Something else altogether to face down a man who just might shoot hell out of you, then stomp your sorry ass like a gob of hocked-up spit.

Ignored the toady and stared right into Pine's lifeless eyes. "You arrogant bastards interrupted my poker game. Whacked a friend of mine across his face for no good reason. Now you're working on bulling everyone in the room, all in less than five minutes. Figure your next move has got to be an effort to intimidate the entire town. Gotta hand it to you boys. You're nervy sons of bitches all right."

He didn't waste any real effort thinking much about a quarrelsome response. Real low, Hector Pine said, "You think you can take all four of us, mister?"

"Way you boys are dressed right now, I could take the four of you and not even break a sweat." Dropped my voice to the point where it sounded like I spoke from the bottom of an empty rain barrel. "Consider this an invitation, Pine. Any of you who wants, just go right ahead and pull one of those smoke wagons. I'll kill the four of you where you stand. First man who moves causes all of you to get dead, right here, right now."

God Almighty, there's nothing like having death walk up and kiss you on the cheek to get a man's attention. Ever so slightly, Pine's eyes flickered. One who called himself Crouch weaved back and forth, started to stammer something, and was waved to silence by his leader. Grizz Jacks looked like a confused child. One-Eyed Frank had the red-faced appearance of a man whose head might explode from an overabundance of uncontrolled thought.

Pine said, "Don't think I got your name, mister."

"Deacon Moon," I lied.

"We ain't never heard of you neither," snapped Crouch.

"All you need to know about me is that you've disturbed my evening's entertainment, attacked one of my friends, and that I'm the man who will kill you tonight if you push it. Appears to me you boys are on a mission to meet Satan. Way it's raining right now, tomorrow would be a sorry day to get buried. But I can sure as hell make arrangements for your funerals."

One-Eyed Frank mumbled, "Ain't nobody a-buryin' me tomorrow."

I should have let it go, but the Devil got into my mouth again. Said, "Well, Frank, that's a good idea. I can see to it that you don't get buried tomorrow. Might have some friends hang your butt-ugly ass on the hitch rack out front for a week or so. Take a few pictures of you. Make you famous. Wait till you start to rot and stink a bit. Maybe feed your maggoty remains to some pigs."

The one they called Grizz gritted his teeth so loud, it sounded like a squirrel breaking pecans. His massive mitts clenched and unclenched. He pawed at the floor like an angry animal, snorted like a bull, and took a step my direction. Had my belly gun up and shot him in a foot the size of a schoolhouse dictionary so fast, I don't think any of those other jackasses even realized what had occurred at first.

Ole Grizz grabbed his injury as a geyser of blood spewed into the air, and dropped to the floor like a felled tree. He rolled around in the sawdust, peanut shells, and tobacco spit, then went to screaming like a little girl. Bet he knocked over ten or fifteen spittoons, a couple of tables, and God knows how many chairs. The thunderous explosion and cloud of rolling smoke finally got the others looking my way.

By the time the poor stunned yahoos glanced up from their wounded friend, I had both pistols out, cocked and ready to deal out some real pain. Took everything I could do to keep from making good on my earlier promise.

Sweet Jesus, but I wanted to kill the hell out of those sorry wretches more than anything I'd wanted in a long time. And I seriously considered mowing them down like ripe wheat.

But Reverend Castleberry's most recent sermon still rang in my ears. That past Sunday, he had preached on the joy of Christian forgiveness, and how much closer we moved to the Lord's right hand by having mercy on our enemies.

I had to yell over all the screeching from their wounded friend. "Doctor has an office next to the mercantile across the street. If my aim was true, Grizz should be missing two or three toes. Get him to the doc right now, and most likely he won't have to take your compadre's foot off."

Kept them under the gun as they gathered the wounded beast up and headed for the door. Between Grizz's toes and Red's nose, gory splatter decorated damn near half the floorboards on my end of the saloon. In spite of the demonstration he'd just got of my skills, Hector Pine turned as his gang reached the door and said, "This ain't the end of it, Moon. We'll be back."

Laughed when I said, "Well, at least one of you'll be on crutches. Take my advice, Pine, do your drinking at the Red Light. Stay out of the Palace. Otherwise, I'll be forced to finish what you bastards started here tonight."

Funny thing about shooting people. The act has a tendency to make other folks afraid of you once word gets around you're capable of dealing out death, or anything close to it. My new friends looked at me differently after that night's event. Treatment became more deferential. Men I'd never spoken with tipped their hats on the boardwalk. Women hid their faces behind fans and skittered away. More than a few of Mexia's residents even seemed afraid of me, which is not at all what I ever wanted.

I cannot blame them for their obvious feelings or unspoken questions, because the incident in the Palace simply announced the beginnings of worse things to come. I had sincerely hoped Pine and his bunch would reconsider the threat he'd made and leave town once their foot-shot amigo received proper medical care. Unfortunately, my heartfelt wishes never saw the light of a peaceful day.

The Pine gang took up semipermanent residence at the Red Light Saloon, and menaced anyone passing from chairs they placed on the boardwalk out front. And for the next two months, hardly a day passed that another incident in a litany of brutality didn't surface that could be laid at their evil feet. Worst of all, their bullying behavior began to have an unfavorable effect on me.

Cletis Hooper, a cowhand from the Double D Ranch, probably put it best. He came in one day, had a beer on me, and said, "Folks are afraid to associate with you any longer, Deacon. We've got badmen roaming our streets that have no hesitation dealing out punishment for being seen with you, and no law to correct the problem. Hell, I might well be taking my life in my own hands for drinking this beer."

Turned over another card in my endless solitaire game and said, "Any of them bother you yet, Cletis?"

"No, but that don't mean much. That one-eyed son of a bitch caught Banker Willis on the street yesterday and pistol-whipped the hell out of him. They's been other such incidents that involved men who've sat at this table. Hell, you're aware of them. Sooner or later, one of those evil bastards will kill someone. If that ain't a lead-pipe cinch, you can piss in my hat and I'll eat it, band, feathers, and all."

Leaned back in my chair and threw my cards on the table. "Thing that puzzles me is why Pine and the rest don't just get it over with and brace me. I'm easy enough to find. So far, they've not so much as directed a wayward word at me since I shot three of their idiot friend's toes off."

As he carefully rolled a handmade, Cletis said, "You know how roving toughs are, Deacon. They always pick on the folks that most likely won't fight back." He lit up and went on between puffs. "Far as the Pine boys are concerned, you've already proved you're a dangerous man. Gonna take a spell of hounding the hell out of others before they grow enough nerve to confront you again."

Laid awake that night and thought it all out. I'd been in Mexia going on nine months, and hated the prospect that I might have to leave. Most part of two years had passed since I'd gone running. Liked my tiny spot of peaceful life. Didn't cotton much to giving it up. I especially hated the prospective loss of a moneymaking game in a friendly establishment, and willing girls from the church who liked to visit me in my hotel room on moonless nights.

But something had to be done. Since just about everyone considered me responsible for the town's unwarranted persecution, I came to the conclusion that Hector Pine and all his cronies would have to die. Hell, I was just the man who could put them in the ground, and from all available evidence, virtually everyone in town expected me to do exactly that.

Next morning, I visited Charlie Harlan's store and purchased two short-barreled coach guns and several boxes of shells. He eyeballed me in a kind of strange way and said, "Never sold a man two at the same time, 'less he planned on riding shotgun for a stage line."

"Well, Charlie," I said, "I don't plan to guard mail or gold shipments. Gonna use these big poppers to get rid of a nest of rats."

He smiled. "Nasty critters, ain't they?"

"They are at that, and I plan to clean 'em out."

Sat down that night after a profitless evening at the Palace, dismantled each of my pistols, then carefully cleaned, oiled, and tuned them to deadly perfection. Packed all my other gear, stretched out, and got myself a good night's sleep.

Dressed in one of my new black suits. Had a fine breakfast the next morning. Went back to my room and took a nap. Half hour before noon, I awoke refreshed and ready to do the Lord's work. Glanced out my hotel window before I headed for the street. Spotted Manfred Crouch and Frank Troy in chairs propped against the wall on either side of the Red Light's entrance. Couldn't see Pine or Jacks, but it didn't matter. Pine rarely came out of the Red Light, and I had no doubt that as soon as I'd killed the two on the boardwalk, their friends would show up.

Hefted a shotgun in each hand and made my way to the boardwalk. Propped the big blasters against the wall. Grabbed the first kid who passed. Said, "You want to make a dollar, son?"

"Sure. But could you tell me what I have to do for it first?"

Handed him the coin and said, "Easy work. Go up and down the boardwalk. Tell any of the town folk you meet that Deacon Moon said for everyone to get off the street."

He rolled the coin in his fingers. "That all?"

"Stay away from the Red Light. Don't say anything to the men out front. Got it, son?"

"Yes, sir, I got it."

Pulled me up a chair and watched as the ragged scamp tore off running. Took him almost twenty minutes, but once the word got to spreading, Crouch and One-Eyed Frank soon found themselves on the street alone. Death was coming after them, and the poor bastards were too stupid to understand why they were almost the only living people on the street.

Soon as all but the most inquisitive town folk cleared out, I grabbed those shotguns, cocked both barrels on each of them, stepped into the street, and headed for whatever awaited me in the Red Light.

Two ignorant sons of bitches on the boardwalk didn't even notice me until I stopped in the street right in front of them. Thought at the time that if One-Eyed Frank's blind eye had been working, the whole deal might have played out some different. As it was, I couldn't have been more than fifteen feet from them when Crouch snapped to attention and jumped to his feet. One-Eyed Frank quickly followed.

Crouch said, "Damned lot of artillery you're a-carryin' today, Moon."

Frank's only eye bugged out like a frog that some mean-assed kid had just stomped on. He grunted, "What the hell you up to, Deacon?"

Brought both those twelve gauges up at the same time and said, "You should have left after I shot Grizz. But did you? No. You've been hanging around here for weeks making folks miserable, and now your time has run out. In fact, all the time God allotted you amongst the living is gone, boys. You're staring into the face of your own deaths. I'm here to kill you fellers."

Manfred Crouch must have owned about two or three

more ounces of brains than his companion. Still and all, he had trouble coming to a decision. When he finally did, an uncertain hand darted toward the pistol on his hip. All I can say about the thing is that he needed to be a damned sight faster.

I snapped both barrels of buckshot on him at the same time. Deafening blast blew so much of his sorry hide onto the Red Light's sun-bleached wall, it looked like someone had applied a real sloppily spattered paint job. Scarlet-tinted chunks of muscle, bone, and guts dripped down the shot-riddled boards and splashed onto the seat of his vacant chair. He squealed like a pig being butchered when all that shot hit him. Then he flopped around like a beached fish for about five seconds. Slung blood, and more gory parts and pieces, all over the place.

Pitched the used-up shooter aside and turned on One-Eyed Frank. He appeared shocked, amazed, and completely dumbfounded. Such events were not of his understanding. In Frank's pathetic world, no one living would have nerve enough to confront, challenge, and then kill one of his closest friends and boon companions. Man went to quaking all over like someone in the throes of a serious shivering fit of deadly ague.

He held out hands that quivered and shook in a beseeching motion and yelped, "Wait. Oh, God. Please don't kill me."

"Too late for begging, Frank. Time to die. Ask God to forgive you for your sorry ways. You've got two seconds."

"Sweet Jesus," he yelped.

"Good choice of last words," I said.

Didn't wait for him to draw. Hell, I didn't wait for him to twitch a finger in the direction of his pistol. Dropped both hammers on him as well. Damn near cut the sorry bastard in half. He was dead before he hit the dusty board-walk planks. To this day, I'm not for certain whether the buckshot killed him or whether I scared him to death. Let the shotgun slip to the ground, pulled both my pistols, and headed for the Red Light's batwing doors.

Stopped outside, stepped to the right, and peered inside
long enough to let my eyes adjust to the saloon's interior
gloom. Hector Pine sat at a table at the far end of a room
shaped exactly like the Palace. Got to hand it to the man.
He didn't appear the least bit affected by all the gunfire
I'd just set loose on his men. Thing that bothered me a bit
was the absence of Grizz Jacks. Man was nowhere to be
seen.

Pushed through the batwings and headed straight for
Pine. Hadn't taken but about two steps when, quicker than
a rattlesnake can strike, his right hand flashed into view.
A deafening shot lit the room. Hot slug burned within
an inch of my head and nicked my right ear. If I hadn't
moved to the left about three inches, I do believe he would
have drilled me right in the nose.

Cut loose with both pistols exactly the way Cutter
taught me. Poker chips, cards, and chunks of wood flew
into the air in a blizzard of wreckage that came back down
like rain in a cyclone. Pine flipped his table over and used
the pitiful thing as a shield. He didn't help his losing
cause much. I kept walking his direction and thumbed one
off for every step I took.

After that initial flurry, the famed gunfighter never fired
another shot. Found him on the floor all chewed up from
at least four of the big ole .45 slugs that smashed through
his ill-conceived protection and bored holes in his worthless, hell-destined hide.

Three of Pine's gushing wounds looked fairly puny to
me. The one that counted hit him in the upper chest just
left of the breastbone. Bright red blood bubbled from his
quaking lips as I eased around for a closer look at my
handiwork. A fist of iron grasped the dripping shirt where
the deadliest bullet pierced him.

Wandering eyes blinked at me. He gasped, "Who the
hell are you?" Long pause before he continued. "Never
heard of no Deacon Moon. You're nothin', nobody, from
out of nowhere."

His eyes closed, and I thought he'd passed. About decided to walk away, but they snapped open again and he said, "Now, you done went and kilt me. Hector Pine, famous Texas gunfighter who dispatched more men than Ben Thompson, kilt by a nobody. It ain't right. Goddammit, it ain't fair." Then God grabbed ole Hector and flung his sorry soul to Hell's front gate.

Reloaded before I sauntered around to the other side of the Red Light's abandoned bar and picked out a fine-looking bottle of whiskey. Poured me a double. Took my time drinking it. Kept thinking maybe ole Grizz would show up, but he never did. As he appeared to have a few nuts loose in his thinker assembly, I was actually reluctant to kill the man. That's why I shot him in his foot in the first place, rather than put him in the ground.

Year or so later, I heard as how one of those toes I removed had got infected. Seems he'd been laid up in their camp outside of town the day I killed all his pardners. Way the tale went, ole Grizz died about a month later from the festering. Might have been better all the way around if I'd shot him.

As time passed, and my reputation became known to friends I'd made in Mexia, many of them decried my actions of that day. Some even went so far as to charge that poor ole Hector and his saintly friends had been foully murdered by a man beset with demons and cursed of God. Such talk cut me to the bone. Way I had it figured, those good citizens were freed from a murderous bondage as surly as Moses delivered God's people out of Egypt. Suppose the lesson I learned was that you just can't please anyone, and when you try, the bastards will turn on you the first chance they get.

I slipped out of Mexia within a week of killing those fellers. Must admit I hated to leave. Had really enjoyed my stay. For the next six months, I lived the way Cutter showed me. Purchased a damned good mule named Beulah, bought the required necessities, tried to avoid towns, and laid low. How was I to know that La Honda Marshal Tom Bankston had put out posters on every tree in South

Texas for me, and that Rangers all over the state were looking to kill Eli Gault—or see to it he swung from the nearest tree. Spilled another bucketful of blood before I found out.

12

"Oh, please, Nathan. Don't kill me."

Whole deadly mess started when I woke up one morning, after having lived on the ground for months, and decided it was way past time to spend a few days sleeping in a real bed. A serious bath, clean sheets, rugs on the floor, shades on the windows, some good whiskey, and perhaps a poker game or two, became something of an obsession. I'd been ambling in a general southerly direction for most of my travels, and decided to pull up in *Cuero*. Town was about the right size—small—and sported the basic amenities I required to satisfy all the itches I felt it necessary to scratch.

Saw to my animals first. Got me a hotel room, a bath, mighty good café-cooked meal, and purchased all the supplies required if called upon to make a hasty departure. Then I headed for the nearest saloon. The fellowship and stimulus of a friendly game of poker awaited just inside a set of batwing doors.

Afternoon started out right pleasant. No professional gamblers in evidence. Had the resident cardsharps to myself. Couple of local wranglers, a friendly whiskey drummer, and a pair of bored locals sat in on the game. Didn't take long to realize none of them were any match for me. But I held back on skinning them. Won a few, lost a few. Gained on those fellers just enough so it didn't bother them too much.

About the time the sun started going down, a real good-looking black-haired gal showed up. Dark-eyed, fiery-lipped, shaped just the right way to make a man want to slap his mama. I saw her when she slipped in the door and kind of edged her way around the wall in my direction. Could tell she was sizing up the potential business. She spotted me from the get-go and, being as how I'd avoided the company of woman for a spell, I made no effort to discourage her attentions.

Said her name was Ruby. Hell, that was all I needed to know. She sat behind me for about two hours and drank anything I wanted to buy. Every once in a while, she'd lean over, breathe into my ear, let an overanxious hand wander up my leg, and whisper something like, "There's a clean room upstairs, good-lookin'. Big feather bed. Bartender lets me use it when gentlemen like you come to town." Or, "Come on, honey. Leave the cards. Let Ruby show you a good time."

Well, didn't take a lot of such behavior to get me going. Quicker'n a Texas twister can snuff a match, got to feeling like I had a crowbar in my pocket. Apologized to the other players and excused myself. They all grinned, made shooing motions like they completely understood my situation and the glorious time to be had with that hot-blooded gal.

Couldn't believe it, but the bartender stopped us as we headed for the stairs and made me sign a hotel register. Said it was required by the state. Hell, by that point, my randiness knew no bounds. I would've gladly put my John Henry to a contract with Satan for my immortal soul just for a few minutes alone with that heavy-breathing, big-breasted gal. Put myself down as Henry Moon in his book and let Ruby lead me to her place of passionate business.

Barely got the door closed when that gal jumped on me like a panther in heat. Went to ripping at my clothes. Everything ended up in a pile on the floor beside the bed. My God, but she was one talented whore. Bounced me around that well-used bed like a snot-nosed kid trying to ride the toughest bucker on the ranch. Good Lord, but I do believe to this very instant she had the most talented tongue I've ever come across. Had a way of licking my ear that had me hooting like a barn owl.

We'd barely finished up, and were about to discuss finances and such, when the door slammed open. Big towheaded son of a bitch carrying an old Walker Colt busted into the room raving like a lunatic. Raised both hands like a man being robbed by a dangerous highwayman.

He stomped over to the end of the bed, waved his antique pistol around in my face, and yelled, "How dare you take advantage of my wife, sir. You've spoiled the spotless reputation of a good Christian woman. By tomorrow morning, everyone in Cuero will have learned of her fall from the Lord's grace." Then, he turned on Ruby for a second. "We have children at home who've been degraded by your depraved and wanton behavior, woman. How could you destroy the Becker name and ruin our family's reputation in the community in such a whorish manner? May God have mercy on you for such sluttish activities."

Ruby had snatched the bedcovers up to hide her brazen nakedness. Tears rolled down lust-tinted cheeks as she whimpered, "Oh, please, Nathan. Don't kill me. How could our poor babies grow up shamed with the death of their mother on their innocent heads? I was only trying to get enough money to help save the ranch."

While I had absolutely no idea at the time what in the green-eyed hell the old badger game involved, I knew something didn't ring true with any of what I was hearing.

The whole affair sounded too much like one of Pa's sermons on the evils of sinful behavior and Satan's eventual
collection of the debt. Hell, I got the sneaking feeling that
just any moment someone would pass the plate and ask
me to grab my pants off the floor and pony up whatever I
could for a love offering.

Sure enough, Nathan Becker did exactly that when he
stared at his randy wife, assumed a profoundly pathetic
look, and said, "Well, my darlin', I suppose forgiveness
would be the Christian thing all right." Then he turned on
me again. Shook that five-pound man blaster in my face
and said, "Your seduction of my formerly chaste spouse
will remain a heinous event in my memory, sir. It will
most certainly scar my heart for years to come, and heap
shame upon the heads of our blameless children. But I
think pardon might be the order of the day. That is, if you
can come up with three hundred dollars to assuage the
grief and humiliation visited upon my fledgling family."

Incredulous, I said, "Three hundred dollars?"

"Yes, by God. And if not, I will be forced to kill you
for the adulterous behavior the two of you have engaged
in this very night. Hell, there ain't a court in Texas would
convict me of your bloody death." Ruby immediately
went to bawling like a stray calf.

So, the big, ugly cat had finally escaped the proverbial
bag. An evening of innocent pleasure, which started out as
a two-dollar romp in the sack with a brazen strumpet, had
somehow transformed itself. Now, I was faced with a
three-hundred-dollar payment to soften the anguish and
disgrace of a devoted mother and wife led astray—led
astray by me, no less. And if I didn't come up with the
money, Nathan Becker intended to shoot me like a rutting
pig. Didn't take long for me to think that one over.

Tried to sound pitiful and repentant when I said, "I am
most willing to pay, sir. Have no desire to die in a bed that
still reeks with the musk of unbridled passion." Looked
for something in the way of a wince, grimace, or recoil

when I referred to the blatant humping his wife had so recently slapped on me. Nothing there. Not so much as a batted eye. "May I retrieve my pants, Mr. Becker?"

"No tricks, you infernal wife seducer," he snapped.

"The money's sewn into the waist of my trousers, Mr. Becker. I'll have to cut it out."

He flipped the pistol barrel at me two or three times, and said, "All right, go ahead, but attempt no tricks, sir. I'm watching, and will have no compunction about blasting trenches in your head at the first sign of treachery."

Slowly leaned over the edge of the bed and made out as though I intended to recover my discarded clothing. Sneaked a peek, from the corner of my eye, as I scratched around in the pile of garments beside the bed. Becker glanced at Ruby and winked. Silly bastard sealed his fate as far as I was concerned. Snatched one of my .45s from beneath the articles of clothing on the floor.

When I came up with the pistol in my hand, the surprised shakedown artist looked like the most astonished man alive. The shocked expression on his stupid face lasted for about a second. Just long enough for me to pull the trigger and blast a blue whistler right between his eyes. Slug punched a finger-sized hole in front of his thick skull. Left a second the size of a guinea egg in back when it exited. Blood, bone, hair, and brains splattered the wall behind him like someone had thrown a bucket of paint against it.

Becker dropped straight to the floor like a gunnysack of rancid cow manure. Ruby went to screeching so loud, people must have heard her in San Antone. Holes in her stupid husband's head sent geysers of hot blood a foot into the air, and sprayed all over everything that wasn't already drenched. Hell of a mess.

Squealing woman hopped out of bed with the sheet still wrapped around her naked body, fell on poor stupid Nathan's lifeless carcass, and sobbed like the world had just ended. I jumped into my pants, grabbed another gun just in time to greet the bartender and several of the players from the poker table at my door.

Cocked both pistols and motioned the armed whiskey slinger inside. He carried an ax handle and looked ready to use it on me at the first opportunity. Son of a bitch stood over the oozing body as Ruby continued to wail and said, "You have any idea what you've done, mister?"

The question struck me as somewhat dim-witted. "Know exactly what I did. Stupid jackass kicked my door in, confronted me with a pistol, threatened my life, and tried to rob me of three hundred dollars. You boys had to have heard the racket from the breakage of the door when he rendered the frame to a pile of splinters, but I didn't see any of you rush up to help me out. So I felt compelled to shoot the bastard before he shot me."

Bartender pointed at Becker's corpse with his ax handle. "This man was the brother of Texas Ranger Tiger Jim Becker."

"Never heard of him," I snapped.

He shook the ax handle at me. "Well, you will, you murderin' son of a bitch. Tiger Jim's a man killer of the first water. He keeps an office right here in town. Ole Tige will have your *cojones* on a flaming stick before you know what's happened."

About then, Ruby sprang off the floor like a branded bobcat and jumped on me with all claws out and working. A few minutes before, she'd used them to urge me into the throes of ecstasy. Now, the crazed woman wanted my eyeballs spiked to the end of her fingertips. Put up with about five seconds worth of it, and finally, had to tap her on the noggin with one of my pistol barrels. She went to ground like a wounded dove.

Pair of yahoos in the doorway leapt across the threshold and started grabbing for their smoke wagons. I ripped off three or four shots, and put both of them down before they'd managed to take two steps.

Black-powder smoke was on the verge of making it impossible to see more than a foot or two. The noise level had almost deafened me. While I was busy with the idiots from the doorway, the crazed whiskey slinger jumped over Ruby, burst through the curtain of spent powder, and whacked me on the side with his club. I ricocheted off the wall behind the bed, turned, and blasted him into the next world as he raised the stick for another attempt at knocking a sizable hole in my head.

Figured all that gunfire would surely stir up the entire town. Didn't help that some of the local poker klatch had survived, taken to their heels, and were in the process of rousing the citizenry by yelling their fool heads off. Grabbed up all my belongings, dropped them out the window, and quickly followed.

Slipped down an alley to the livery and retrieved Beulah and my horse. Managed to get out of town alive, and hightailed it for Laredo. Hoped my good luck would hold and that the chuckleheads from Cuero, like Tiger Jim, had seen the last of Eli Gault. But it was wishful thinking on my part. It's been my experience that when events start going bad, nothing but blood can stop them.

Late the next afternoon, I reined up on a rise east of the San Antonio River. Low, scrub-covered country rolled back toward Cuero. Pulled my long glass, and quickly spotted rising dust some miles away. Figured Ranger Tiger Jim Becker had managed to raise a posse, and that the angry mob intended to hang me from the nearest mesquite tree at the earliest possible opportunity.

Watched the pale powder rise for about ten minutes, then decided the posse was traveling at a pretty good clip, and would most likely have me under their guns by the next morning. Started right that very moment searching for a good place to lay an ambush. Firmly believed I would likely have to kill a few in order to turn the loosely constituted group of farmers and shopkeepers back toward hearth and home. Tiger Jim, however, posed another problem altogether.

Crossed the shallow river and found a rocky hill that gave me a great range of fire. Determined I would wait till my pursuers got to the west side with me, and then open up on them. Reasoned as how wranglers and shopkeepers don't have much real fight in them. Figured if I got lucky enough to put one or two of those boys down, the rest would retreat.

Found the perfect spot to hide. Forted up behind a pile of covering boulders and laid out both my Winchesters, along with plenty of shells. Had to wait almost two hours before I detected movement on the far side of the river. Watched them through the long glass.

Counted nine men. Appeared to me as though more than half the party had no inclination to continue their pursuit across the river. But after some considerable discussion, a feller with droopy mustaches, who wore a huge palm-leaf hat and faded bib-front shirt, led the party across. Thought to drop him right off. Felt he was most likely the famed Texas Ranger, Tiger Jim Becker. His plan of attack complicated my earlier ideas. Decided I couldn't wait for everyone to cross over, if I wanted to get him out of the way first.

Waited till Becker's horse set foot on my side of the river before I fired my first shot. Winchester boomed, and sent rattling echoes up and down the river. Unfortunately, the Ranger's clumsy beast stumbled, and I hit the second feller's animal dead center. Thought to myself, damned if you aren't one lucky son of a bitch, Tiger Jim.

Floundering beast caused just enough confusion in the posse for me to put death-dealing shots in two of the fellers behind Tiger Jim. Wounded at least three others before their panicked compadres managed to hide themselves behind trees and rocks along the San Antonio's rough bank.

Lots of befuddled yelling back and forth as the fractured posse tried to figure out where the shots originated. Heard one feller yell, "Butch and Greeley are dead, Jim. We've got others what are badly wounded."

Spotted the feller doing the yelling, and put a blistering shot through his sugar-loaf sombrero—hard to miss a target that big. Had hoped to nick some of the head inside, but I hurried my shot. Only damaged the silly goober's hat. His fellow sons of bitches cussed me for all they were worth. Torrent of the bluest language imaginable surged up the hill and washed over me like the overflow from a flash flood. Set me to laughing. Knew them boys were whipped and more than ready to give up the fight.

But one of them must have spied the gun smoke coming from my hidey-hole. Hot lead started falling around me like hailstones during a thunderstorm. Blasting went on for a good twenty minutes. I sent them back as good as I got. Even managed to hit another of the stupid jackasses when he jumped up and made a run for Tiger Jim's position. Ranger had concealed himself behind a cottonwood that would have hid a stagecoach. Situation got considerable quiet after the runner went down.

Something close to half an hour must have passed with little movement and no gunfire leveled in my direction. I could hear the posse members yelling back and forth, but the wind had begun to swirl and it became harder to grasp exactly what they said at times. Most of them seemed of the opinion that they'd suffered heavily and might need to turn back to Cuero before some of their wounded passed on.

Finally, heard shouting I could make out. "Mr. Moon, this is Ranger Tiger Jim Becker speaking. You've done went and shot the hell out of my posse. We've got several dead. A number of others are wounded. Let us take our leave and I promise to give you a five-day head start before resuming the search."

Hollered back, "Why should I agree to such a deal, Ranger? Got you boys under my guns, and can probably kill every single one of you. Might take a day or two, but I've got plenty of time."

An uneasy quiet descended for a minute or so. Then Tiger Jim came back with, "Men are suffering down here. You're bound to have a little Christian mercy in some small corner of your murderous black soul, Mr. Moon.

Allow me to lead my living friends back to town for proper care, and I promise to deal with your sorry ass at a later date."

Well, that one really set me to laughing. Guess my response must have unnerved ole Tiger Jim. He went to cussing me for all he was worth. But being as how he'd tickled my funny bone some, and being as how I wanted to be on my way, I hollered down at him, "Take 'em home, Jim. Promise to hold my fire and will bind you to yours of a five-day lead. But be advised, I will kill you when next we meet."

Last thing he said was, "Being as how you've already put my brother in the ground, I look forward to that God-sent day with great anticipation, sir."

Took the remaining fellers who could still boast of good health a spell to gather up their wounded, get loaded, and start back for Cuero. Tiger Jim brought up the rear of his fractured group. I watched until he got to the east side of the San Antonio. Beaten Ranger whirled his dun horse around and shook a gloved fist at me. Jumped up on the rock I hid behind and waved like he was the prodigal son returning home to the open arms of a grateful brother.

Must've really made him mad. He hopped down, kicked rocks into the water, shook his fist some more, and yelled something I couldn't make out. Put on quite a display. Got me to thinking maybe ole Tiger Jim wasn't the kind to make idle threats. Figured I'd better make the best of my five-day head start and burn leather.

For the first time since I'd taken a shovel to Pa's evil noggin, I had an uneasy feeling about the future. Never had worried much about staying alive before Tiger Jim showed up in my life. Think I spent every waking moment from that day till we met again worrying about the bastard. Knew for damned certain when we locked eyes somewhere down the road, I would have to be steady, fast, and accurate, or the man would kill me deader'n a rotted fence post.

Couldn't think of a good way to simply disappear. But then, God stepped in and rescued me again. Happened just outside the tiny village of Beeville. Ran across a branch of the Chisholm Trail, and right into the open arms of Amos Bloodsworth.

13

"Damn near five hundred head drowned."

On the third day after Tiger Jim and I parted company, I reined up on a small rise. Threw a leg over my saddle horn and watched them roll across the countryside like a living wave—thousands of longhorn cattle. That hair-covered ocean took so much time to pass, I climbed down, spread my blanket on the ground under a friendly live oak, and rolled a cigarette.

Cowboy riding flank spotted me and kicked over for a minute to visit. Pulled a dust-covered bandanna away from his sweaty face and said, "Mind if I enjoy your shade for a few seconds, mister?"

Waved him to the coolest spot under the tree. "Not a bit. Help yourself."

He fished tobacco and papers from a battered leather vest, and soon joined me in a relaxing smoke. "Where do you boys hail from?" I asked.

"Casa Blanca. 'Bout fifty miles east of Laredo. Mr. Amos Bloodsworth runs these ornery beasts under the Lazy B brand down that way. He's got three thousand head in this bunch. We're pushin' for the railhead in Dodge."

The depth of my ignorance of cows, cattle drives, and such led to the next question. "How long will it take?"

He scratched his chin, took a drag on the hand-rolled, and said, "Depending of how the weather goes, barring any major accidents, and whether or not we have trouble with Injuns or cattle raiders, should make 'er in three months—give or take a week or two here and there."

Flabbergasted, I said, "Three months? Sweet Jesus, didn't have any idea a drive would take that long."

"Never been out on one of these dances, I take it."

"You take it right, amigo. I've wanted to try my hand at one, but the opportunity never came up. Besides, doubt I have the skills necessary for such work."

He laughed. "Don't need much in the way of skill to push these poor dumb critters. Just have to take your time. Don't want to urge 'em along too fast."

"Why not?"

"Well, faster they move, the more weight they lose. You've gotta let 'em find their own pace—ten, maybe twelve miles a day."

Spotted the drag riders bringing up the end of the herd and grabbed my blanket. "Nice talking with you. Kinda wish I could go along to Dodge."

He leaned over and locked me in a squinty gaze. "Oh, you can. We lost a man just six days from the ranch. Poor son of a bitch got bit by the damnedest rattlesnake I've ever seen. As big around as ole Cookie's skinny leg, and almost six feet long. Kilt poor Junior Jefferies deader'n the doorknob on a Kansas City whorehouse so quick, none of us could believe it."

I hated snakes and couldn't help asking, "Merciful Father. How'd he get bit?"

"Poor bastard bent down to pick up his bedroll one morning. Snake must have been sleepin' under the blanket somewheres. Jumped all of five feet and bit Junior on the side of his neck." He pointed to a spot under his left ear.

"We had to pry that snake off'n him. Boy died in less than an hour. He'd only seen seventeen summers. Sorry-assed shame if you ask me."

Tied the bedroll behind my saddle and got mounted again. Was about to pull away when he said, "I'll take you to Mr. Bloodsworth, if you'd like. Sure he'll hire you. Any hand's always better'n none, or a dead one. Won't take long to learn cowboy'n for any man who can ride. Hell, I'll teach you."

"Well, I can ride, but my talent doesn't really involve horses or cows."

He appeared confused. "What exactly is your talent, sir?"

"Guns," I said, "and the deadly use of them."

He pushed a frazzled straw hat to the back of his head, stared at the weapons on my hip and across my belly. "Well, that's even better'n bein' able to ride and rope where we're goin'. Once we get to the north side of the Red, might need a man of your abilities. What's your name?"

"Eli Gault."

"Well, Eli, Mr. Bloodsworth is gonna love havin' you along for the ride. Come with me."

Amos Bloodsworth had more than a little in common with a grizzly bear. He lumbered my direction when I climbed down next to the chuck wagon, and checked me over like his next meal had just arrived in camp.

He pawed at a hair-covered chin and glanced at my guide. "See you've done went and found a stray, Boots."

Boots motioned my direction. "Mr. Bloodsworth, this here's Eli Gault." The Casa Blanca rancher removed a battered glove and offered a paw for me to shake.

Boots grabbed a pair of empty cups. Handed me a full tin of the hot stump juice and spoke as he poured. "Yessir. Being as how Junior went under, thought you might want to talk with this feller, Mr. Bloodsworth. He's possessed of a talent I think you might find interestin'."

Bloodsworth's gaze shifted back to me. Made me feel

like a two-headed chicken in a traveling sideshow. "What talent might that be, stranger?" I thought him mighty formal, being as we were at least fifty miles from the nearest town.

"As I told Boots, guns. And the deadly use of them."

"Guns?"

"Yes indeed. I'm hell on wheels with pistols in my hands—about as good as it gets."

Bloodsworth laid heavily muscled arms that strained at the seams on a cotton work shirt across his chest, kind of leaned back on his heels, and eyeballed me. "Is that a fact? You're that good, huh?"

"Would you like a demonstration?" He'd stepped on more than a few of my toes. Guess my answer came out a shade on the crotchety side.

"No. No. Don't need you to take no test. You say it's so, I believe you, son." Cupped his chin with the palm of the hand I shook, and gave me another thorough looking-over. "Wuz just wonderin' if you're on the run by any chance."

Smiled at him and said, "Could be. My personal problems shouldn't matter one way or the other to anyone here. I can be extremely helpful if trouble arises along the trail. Hostiles, cattle raiders, thieves, killers, or miscreants of any kind give you a problem, and you'll be pleased to have me along."

"Ever done any cowboyin' before, Eli? Been on any trail drives? Know anything about cattle?"

"To be absolutely truthful, I'd have to answer no to all of your questions. But I can do this." Poured the coffee out of my cup and tossed it into the dust about fifteen feet in front of me. Had my guns drawn, cocked, and ready to fire—so fast Bloodsworth almost passed out.

In a panic, the rancher motioned with both hands for me to hold off. He hissed, "Don't fire them pistols, son, please. We'd have to chase this herd all the way to Fort Worth before they stopped. You can show me how good a shot you are later."

Did one of Cutter's fancy spins, and returned my pistols to their holsters. "Does that mean I'm hired?"

"You're hired. Thirty dollars a month and found is the usual for a run-of-the-mill cowboy. I'll pay you the same, but will raise it to fifty if your special talents are ever needed. That acceptable?"

Smiled when I said, "Sounds fine to me, sir." We sealed the bargain with spit and a handshake.

He pointed a lazy finger at my guide. "Boots will take you in tow. Teach you as much as you're able to learn about bein' a cowhand. Can stow your gear in the chuck wagon or leave it on your mule. Probably better if you stowed it—easier on the mule anyway. Grab a plate. Cook's just about got meat and beans ready."

Figured taking a job with the Lazy B served a good purpose. Nowhere else to hide out came to mind. Besides, stringing along with Bloodsworth's drive offered me a fine way to cover my trail, and perhaps keep Tiger Jim from finding me. The pay was of no consequence. An oilskin wrapper inside my saddlebag covered more than ten thousand dollars I'd saved from my roguish travels as a gambler. And so, as simple as pie, that's the way I happened to become a cowhand headed for Dodge City, Kansas—and, more important, how a reputation finally caught up with me.

After supper that first afternoon, Boots came to me with a stack of well-used clothing and a saddle that had seen better days. He dropped them beside me. "Fancy suit of clothes you're wearing just won't do out here, Eli. Got some of the boys to chip in a few things that'll make the work a lot easier. Be sure to wear the chaps and gloves, even if you can't use anything else I brought. Brush can cut right through a pair of canvas pants. Gloves'll save your hands."

"What about my animals, Boots?"

He hitched a thumb at the cook. "I checked with Cookie. You can tie 'em to the back of the chuck wagon during the day, or run 'em in our remuda. Don't mean no disrespect, but your horse is pretty much useless for the kinda work we do. Have to ride one of our cow ponies. Your saddle's a shade on the fancy side, too. Way too heavy." He toed at the one he'd brought. "This ole Denver's almost worn out, but not quite. Better if you use it. They's a long, hard day comin' tomorrow, Eli. Best get some sleep if you can. The cook'll have us up and around at first light."

The next few weeks remain in my memory as an agonizing blur of bone-jarring hard work, damned little sleep, and constant attention from Boots McGraw. Hardest lesson I had to learn involved staying horsed on one of those cow ponies. Damned animals could change directions so fast, I got thrown about a dozen times before finally adjusting to their speed and skill.

Second toughest involved a roping technique called the head-and-heel catch. Didn't have too much trouble with the head, but heelin' proved almost as mysterious to me as the origins of the universe. Good way to lose a thumb real fast, too.

But eventually, all the pieces of the cowboy puzzle began to fall into place. By the time we reached Fort Worth, I'd worked every position in the drive formation—point, swing, flank, and drag. Worst of it was riding drag. Wouldn't recommend the job to anyone as a way to make a living. Longest, dustiest days I've spent in my entire life involved riding drag for the Lazy B.

Mr. Bloodsworth bedded his herd down a little west of Fort Worth. Said he couldn't afford the cost of keeping them penned in the Fort Worth stockyards.

He gathered the crew, once we had everything under control, and said, "Have a schedule written out on this here piece of paper, boys. I'll post it on the chuck wagon. Half of you can visit Hell's Half Acre today, half tomorrow. Then we'll push for the Red River. Git whatever drinkin' and whorin' you've got in mind done on your trip to the Acre. I want everyone on his toes when we get to the Red. Never know just what kind of pickle might present itself at the crossing."

Since I had no understanding of the difficulties we might soon face, popped off and said, "What kind of problems do you mean, Mr. Bloodsworth?"

Sounded to me as though he relished answering the question. Got the impression our boss felt an obligation to prepare those, like me, who'd never had to move a herd across a major river before.

Reminded me of my pa getting ginned up for a sermon when he started with, "Could be easy, Eli. Nothin' to it. Might even wade 'em across that unpredictable stream with no trouble a-tall. Seen it go that way many a time before. Then again, could be like a few years ago when the Red flooded. More'n forty thousand head from a dozen different ranches bunched up on this side waitin' to cross."

Old cowboy named Prentiss Taylor, who looked as ancient as my used-up saddle, chimed in with, "Wuz there for that 'un, Mr. Bloodsworth. Worst day of my life wuz when the crossin' finally started. Ain't never seen such a boogered-up mess in my entire life. Hell, I thought more'n a time or three I wuzn't gonna live out the day."

Bloodsworth nodded and continued. "Flood created one helluva problem. We waited a few days for the river to drop. But then, everyone on this side woke up one morning and tried to push his herd over at the same time. Don't know to this day how they did it, but boys like Prentiss got 'em across. And then, my God, it took weeks to sort 'em all out once we finally arrived on the north bank."

Prentiss slapped his hat against a skinny thigh and said, "Damnedest thing I done ever seen. Hope not to see such again."

Bloodsworth nodded his agreement. "Damn near five hundred head drowned. Cattle was stacked up on the bank like cordwood." Man shook his head, and his chin dropped to his chest as though he was on the verge of tears. Then jerked off his hat and stared at the ground. "Four damned good cowboys perished with 'em. Two of 'em was mine. Never had to bury that many at one time.

So, you boys go have fun, but get yourself ready for the Red."

The boss had me scheduled for an Acre visit that first night. But I went to him and volunteered to stay in camp and work both nights so some of the other drovers could have a little extra fun.

'Course I wasn't simply being a fine feller. I harbored an ulterior motive for my actions. Didn't want to gamble on the chance someone in town might recognize my face and perhaps link me to Cutter and past events. Such an episode could well have proven neck-stretchingly costly.

Bloodsworth didn't care one way or the other. Johnson Pratt, the brush popper whose place I took that second night, was thrilled beyond words. He made me a present of a bottle of whiskey for being so nice.

14

"I'm in the business of killing . . ."

Three weeks and a hundred miles past Fort Worth, the herd drew up on the south side of the Red. Entire crew was allowed two hours to visit the rough-and-tumble village of Red River Station. I sat that one out, too. Figured if any well-known gamblers were about, they might somehow mess around and recognize me.

Most of the boys came back to camp pretty well lit up on rotgut whiskey. They suffered something unmerciful for their fun the next day, but glowingly recalled those stopovers for weeks afterward. Couldn't seem to talk enough about the grand times they'd had in Hell's Half Acre and the Station.

Along the way from Fort Worth, I'd heard more fearsome nighttime stories about what we faced at the crossing. Kid named Terry Reed, whose twelve-year-old appearance belied an experienced hand, lounged by the fire a week or so before our arrival and said, "I done this 'un before, just like Prentiss. Didn't attend the big drownin' he and Mr. Bloodsworth described, but two year ago, I wuz with the Double D outfit from down Victoria way. When we come on the river, she was all swolled out'n her banks with ragin' water from up north. Silly-assed foreman said he didn't care. Got all red in the face and said we had to move them cattle across right by-God immediate."

Youngster next to him looked concerned. "Don't know 'bout you fellers, but I cain't swim. Can you swim, Terry?"

Reed snorted, "Hell, I ain't met a handful of cowboys what can. Anyway, we pushed them poor bawlin' beasts into the river, and everything that can go wrong did go wrong. Lost thirty-some head in less than four hours. Cowboy named Tisdale got snakebit. Cook tried every cure he knowed. Didn't do no good a-tall. Tisdale died a horrible death 'bout a week later. Lot worse than the way Junior bought it. On top of everything else, we spent un-countable hours pulling cows out of the damned quick-sand."

Considerable muttering around the fire came from those like myself who were inexperienced in fording a river like the Red. Reed propped his head in his hand and said, "Gonna have to trust your horse, boys. Pray the river ain't runnin' heavy and brown with water from New Mex-ico and the Panhandle."

Bloodsworth, Boots, and an old hand named Cletis Brainerd scouted the river and came back with good news. Crew gathered around the three men and listened as Boots said, "Looks like we've hit it lucky this time. Red's less than a foot deep all the way across. Should be able to walk 'em over with little or no trouble."

An enthusiastic cheer went up from the crew, but ole Brainerd waved a quieting hand and said, "But don't get careless. Keep your eyes open for snakes and quicksand. Either one of 'em is just as deadly as high water."

Everything went right fine, until Cookie tried to run the chuck wagon across. Somehow, he managed to find a hole with his left rear wheel. Quicksand grabbed the wheel, bogged it down to the hubs, and wouldn't let go. Wagon lurched over so far, the hubs on the right side almost faced the sky. We unloaded everything that could be reached. Didn't help much. When the oxen strained to pull the wagon loose, they twisted the tongue and broke it off. Sounded like a pistol shot when it snapped.

Couple of the men, who could boast at least some skill at woodworking, chopped a cottonwood pole and fashioned a new one. Whole herd had crossed by the time those boys got it attached. Crew spent hours digging around the trapped wheel, and finally dragged the wagon to safety on the north side of the river.

I reined up beside Bloodsworth as he watched the work from horseback. He threw a leg over his saddle horn, rolled a smoke, and took a puff. Turned to me and said, "Man learns pert quick out here that such as this is the way of a cattle drive, Eli. Just when you make the mistake of thinking everything is going along about as well as can be expected, an unforeseen bust-up like this 'un happens."

"Just never know what God has in store for us, Mr. Bloodsworth," I said.

"No, we don't, son. But it sure would be nice if we could get through at least one day without some kind of calamity befalling us."

Suppose he must've prayed on it some. For the next three weeks or so, the days came and went in an exhausting parade of nothing but unparalleled heat, blowing dust, the ass end of tired cattle, and boredom.

Then, late one afternoon about ten miles south of the Washita, I was riding swing when Prentiss stormed up. Man's excitement almost got the best of him. "Boss wants you up front quick as you can get there. Said to bring your guns and be prepared for a fight."

I tried to slow him down some. Said, "Where is he, Prentiss? I need to know exactly where you left him."

Excited brush popper pointed north with a trembling hand. "He's two, maybe three, miles out ahead of the herd. Near half a dozen rough-looking characters done stopped him."

"You know what they want?"

He puzzled over the question for a spell before answering. "Not for certain sure, Eli. But if they's like most of that type, they's after as many of our herd as Mr. Bloodsworth's willing to give up."

"You think they're cattle raiders?"

"Sure looked the part to me."

I kicked hard for the chuck wagon. Had rarely carried my weapons since starting the trip. Wrapped and stowed them away from the dust and weather. Usually cleaned and reloaded the whole set at least once a week. Bloodsworth's call from near the Washita was my first chance to earn the extra money he'd promised.

Got myself armed with everything I owned. Prentiss led the way. Spotted the meeting, and made my nervous guide stay behind. Figured he would just be one more thing to worry about. Five trail toughs carrying guns was plenty.

Reined up beside my boss about the time a greasy, stinking son of a bitch who looked, and smelled, like a buffalo hunter that'd been dragged through a cesspool said, "Well, that ain't good enough, by God. We want at least a thousand head. A hundred wouldn't be worth our trouble. Just might as well make up your mind to the way things are, you Texican bastard. Give us the cows, or we'll scatter your whole herd all over the Nations. Goddamn Injuns'll have all of 'em et 'fore this time next week."

Bloodsworth snuck a glance my direction for about a second. I winked, and he turned back to his tormentor. "Like you to meet Eli Gault. Eli, this bag of puss is Jonas Cisco. Most of the five behind him are his brothers. Think that bald son of a bitch is Bucky Grimsley. Nothin' but thieves, the whole damned bunch. I've had dealings with 'em before on previous drives. But this is the first time they've been bold enough to demand a thousand head to let us pass safely."

Cisco didn't like what he'd heard. "Best watch your mouth, cowman. Hell, mess with me and my hands and I just might take your whole damned bunch. Leave you with nothing but cow chips to pick up on your way back to Texas."

I had ridden up on my own horse carrying all the armament necessary to rub out the whole damned bunch— to my way of thinking anyhow. Big line back dun I rode was impervious to gunfire. Wouldn't so much as twitch should any shooting occur.

Wrapped the dun's reins around my saddle horn. Did it as slowly as I could so as not to alarm the foul-smelling puss bag, or any of his equally ugly, malodorous followers.

Caught Cisco's eye and said, "Problem you've got right now, pardner, isn't how many cows you can get away from here with. Your problem is how you're gonna get away from here alive."

The oily thief eyeballed me for about a second and turned back to Bloodsworth. "Who the hell's this pup? Does he do all the talkin' for you now, mister?"

Amos shifted in his saddle. Could tell he was mighty uncomfortable with the whole situation. "Eli hired on and does a special job of work for me, Bucky."

Cisco, and the four men backing him up shifted their gaze around to me again. "And just what would that be?" he growled.

Smiled, but didn't blink, when I said, "I'm in the business of killing people like you, Mr. Cisco."

He threw me a derisive chuckle. "Hell, boy, you think you can scare me? I've squashed more dung beetles like you than I can count on all ten of my fingers, toes, too. Mess with us, and we'll stake both your stupid Texas asses to an anthill and leave you for the buzzards." Once I'd been dismissed, he turned back to Amos. "Now—give us the goddamned cows."

Well, to my way of thinking, there was no need for the conversation to go any further. So I shot him. Man didn't even have time to be shocked or amazed when the open muzzle of my Colt popped up in his face and delivered a burning-hot chunk of sizzling lead to his grease-covered forehead.

Bullet hole about an inch over his left eyebrow didn't amount to much. But the one in back, where it came out, opened a crater in his skull that splattered all his friends and family with chunks of bone, brain matter, blood, and gore. Fine mist of the stuff put a hint of copper in the air that drifted up my nose and made me grit my teeth. Slug knocked ole Jonas ass over teakettle. His horse bucked and went to hopping around like a bird after a fat june bug. Dead man landed right at the feet of one of the animals behind him.

With a pistol in each hand, I thumbed off rounds at those lined up in front of me—so fast the firing sounded like a Gatling gun going off. Blasted all four of them out of their saddles before they even had time to get a grip on their weapons.

Roar from those long-barreled Colts hadn't yet died away when I stepped down and went about examining the bodies, to make sure I'd for damned certain killed all those two-tailed skunks. First one I came on still breathed. So, I shot him again. Put one right in his worthless noggin. Splattered him all over the ground. Know he was down and couldn't defend himself, but hell, if I'd of let him up, he just might have killed me. Hell of a bloody mess. Blades of grass for fifteen feet in any direction dripped with gore and a variety of body fluids.

Must admit, though, it surprised the hell out of me when that baldheaded joker, the one Amos called Grimsley, jumped up, remounted, and rode away. Snapped off a shot from the hip, but missed him. Ran back to the dun and pulled my Winchester from its boot. Got behind the horse and used the saddle as a rest. Took so long to line up a good shot, the evil scamp got most of a hundred yards away before I fired the last time. Dropped him like a white-tailed buck running through South Texas scrub country.

Big ole .45-60 slug hit the bastard between the shoulder blades. Knocked him over his horse's head like I'd whacked him from behind with a rail-splitting maul.

Guess I must've lost control about then. Laughed out loud when Bucky the badman bit the dust. Glanced over at Bloodsworth. The stricken, flabbergasted look on his face came as something of a surprise. He motioned toward the corpses, opened his mouth—several times—as though he wanted to say something, but nothing came out.

Finally, he stepped off his mount like a man under water, removed his hat, and said, "Sweet merciful Jesus, Eli. I ain't never seen nothin' to match this. Heard of such from fellers what fought in the big war. Just never witnessed this many kilt by one man so quick. Goddamn, son."

Couldn't believe he'd gone soft on me like that. Pointed at the bodies with my pistol and said, "This is what you hired me to do, Amos. What'd you expect? You sent Prentiss for me. Did you believe for a solitary minute that I'd get out here in the middle of nowhere with these thieving killers and try to engage such men in a doily-makin' contest? Came here to kill 'em, and that's exactly what I did."

Guess my harangue must have caused his spine to suddenly reappear. He glared at me and snapped, "Hell, I don't know exactly what I expected. But, good God, killin' five men sure as hell wasn't it. Just thought maybe you could get 'em under the gun and intimidate 'em a bit. Jesus, what're we gonna do with all these bodies?"

Took him by the arm and said, "Get a grip, Amos. This isn't a real problem. If I hadn't drilled all of these fellers, you, and any number of your crew, might've ended up dead. No one will miss this bunch. We'll take their saddles and guns. Then we'll bury them right here where they fell, turn their animals loose, and go on our way."

He looked at me like I'd grown another head. "You can't possibly believe that covering up the killing of five men is that easy, Eli."

"Oh, yessir. Indeed I do. Look, the herd has to pass over this exact site. Once that happy event occurs, even you and I won't be able to find this spot again. In a week or two, the grass will start to grow back. No one will ever be the wiser. Besides, who in hell cares what happens to scum like these? Bet their mothers won't even miss 'em."

So, way it all shook out in the end, me, Bloodsworth, Boots, and Prentiss dug one big shallow hole, dumped all five of those fellers in, and covered them up with about two feet of dirt. We kept their guns and saddles. Turned their horses loose to fend for themselves.

Prentiss watched as the animals headed east. Shook his head and said, "Injuns'll have some of them poor critters roasting over a campfire 'fore tomorrow's sun has a chance to set."

Amos mumbled, "You're probably right, son." Then he stomped to his horse and rode back to the herd.

Didn't have any more trouble from that bloody afternoon until we arrived in Dodge. Couple of poor, starving Indians showed up once. Bloodsworth gave them a steer, which they promptly shot and butchered on the spot. Poor beast still quivered when those unfortunate, desperate folk sliced off thick portions. Ate the meat raw. My God, but it was sad to see a once-proud people reduced to such a pitiable state.

Soon as we crossed the Arkansas and bedded the cattle, the boss paid me off.

At first I couldn't believe it when he said, "Lazy B's no longer in need of your services, Eli."

But truth is, I could tell my continued presence made the man mighty uncomfortable. Word of what transpired with the cattle raiders had spread through the crew in spite of the fact that only four of us knew the whole story. Once again, those friends I'd made started treating me different. Some even avoided me. Life tends to go that way when you become known as a man killer. Hell, I didn't care.

We'd been on the trail for more than two months. Work as a cowboy had proved hard, nasty, and mean. Sipping

Kentucky bourbon, while shuffling the pastboards, sure beat hell out of trailing dogies. Now found myself in the Sodom and Gomorrah of the plains. Wanted me a hot bath, clean clothes, a randy woman, and a warm spot at a poker table.

Hot diggity, damn! Heaven on earth!

15

"I want him dead, dead, dead . . ."

According to some of the older cowboys I'd met while in the employ of Mr. Amos Bloodsworth, Dodge City started life as a dismal collection of mud-daubed log cabins and shabby tents. By 1880, when I arrived, the overall look and feel of the sprawling "Babylon of the plains" had changed considerably. Hotels, saloons, dance halls, barber-shops, general mercantile stores, boot makers, and shoe-makers abounded. Frenzied construction appeared never ending. Hell's fire, a feller could buy anything his heart desired and his pocketbook could stand—from the com-pany of a willing woman to fine Frenchified brandy. My God, what more could an energetic young man with four months salary burning holes in his pants crave?

Arrived in town, got the animals settled, and estab-lished myself on the first floor of a three-story hotel not far from a likely-looking dance hall and gambling estab-lishment named Varieties. Found out later the owner was none other than George Masterson—brother of the famed Bat Masterson.

Staked out a chair at a table near the bar, and immediately went to adding as much as possible to my already thick pile of loot. Found out right quick the number of trail hands eager to throw their hard-earned money away on a bad hand of poker surpassed all my wildest imaginings. By the end of the third week in Dodge, I'd almost doubled my stash.

Got to know just about everyone who was anyone, including the more famous Masterson, during my six-month sojourn there. Gamblers, gunmen, store owners, hotel operators, and lawmen became my boon companions and valued acquaintances. Didn't take me but about a heartbeat to realize the town was almost smothered in an abundance of law, but damned short on anything like order.

My most important social contact, however, wasn't of the hairy-legged category. Nope, had been in town less than a week when a blond-haired, blue-eyed gal named Trixie Calhoun blew so much smoke up my skirt I actually came to believe she cared. Took a while for me to learn the eternal fallacy of such misguided beliefs.

We met during one of my frequent visits to a smaller but nonetheless interesting watering hole named the Lame Dog Saloon. Gal brushed her ample hip against mine, fluttered long eyelashes my direction, and in less time than it'd take to blow out a lamp, we were in my bed humping like crazed weasels. Next morning, she moved all her belongings in, and stayed with me until I left town.

Came to the conclusion there's just nothing like the constant and enthusiastic companionship of a talented woman to make a man feel good. I didn't care if the gal continued to pursue her chosen trade—long as I didn't have to know about it and she didn't use my bed. Hell, had no plans to marry up and make her an honest woman. Besides, I'm still not sure till this very moment that such a possibility actually exists for working girls.

Five months into my Kansas raid, perhaps the oddest event of my entire blood-letting career occurred. A broad-shouldered, rough-hewn cattleman strolled up to me at the bar in Varieties, held out his ham-sized hand, and said, "Name's Titus Butcher, Mr. Gault."

Shook his paw with as much enthusiasm as I could muster. "Glad to make your acquaintance. Appears you've got something on your mind, Mr. Butcher."

"That I do, sir. Arrived in town two days ago with a herd I pushed up from near Corpus Christi." Surprised hell out of me when Butcher suddenly teared up. He jerked a bandanna from his pocket and blew a bulbous nose before continuing. "Three weeks into the Nations, a murderous thug hired especially for this trip by my foreman shot my son to death and ran like a chicken-killin' coyote. My boy was an exceptional young man, only fifteen years old, and did nothing to deserve such a useless death at the hands of a professional killer."

Didn't know the man, or the dead lad, so it took some doing, but I tried to act sympathetic. "Sorry to hear such a sad tale, sir. Heartbreaking when anyone that young meets his Maker. Excuse me for possibly intruding on your obvious grief, but what does your son's passing have to do with me?"

"Story goin' 'round these parts leads me to believe Eli Gault is a deadly adversary when it comes to gunplay. Hear tell you killed more'n a dozen men on the way up from Texas. I'd like to hire you to find the man who murdered my son. Pay is damned good, Mr. Gault."

"Want me to bring your son's murderer to you for arrest by local law enforcement and suitable hanging?"

Butcher was mighty emphatic when he said, "Don't want him brought in. I want him dead, dead, dead, and from what I've been given to understand, you're the one man in Dodge who can satisfy my request." He threw down a full shot of gator sweat, then fixed me in a hard gaze.

Most logical question I could've asked came up next. "Why don't you go after him yourself?"

No hesitation. He came back with, "I raise cattle for a

living, Mr. Gault. Only experience I have with guns involves gettin' rid of varmints. This particular pest carries a reputation for deadly use of firearms and a total lack of conscience. No false pride at stake by admitting that I'm no match for him."

"What makes you think I'm a match for him?"

"Reputation, sir. Been hearing about you since before I left home. Eli Gault's growing legend has spread from the piney woods of the great Lone Star State, west to San Antone and beyond. When Brady Pike murdered Titus Junior, I knew beyond any doubt you'd be the man to seek out. Fortunate for me you're still in Dodge."

Figured humble and law-abiding was the best tack with Butcher. I'd tried to keep out of trouble's way since arriving in the cattle capital of the West. So I said, "Can't just go around killing anyone handy, you know—even if the pay is good and the potential victim as guilty as mark-ed Cain."

He leaned forward, fished a star-shaped deputy sheriff's badge, and some official-looking pieces of paper from his jacket pocket. Laid the pile on the bar. Pushed it all my direction. Anxious cowman lowered his voice to a whisper. "I've had *financial* consultations with representatives of the local constabulary. What you have here is an official deputy's commission, letters of introduction to any trail bosses you might encounter who could assist when necessary, and a legal warrant for Pike's arrest— which I fully expect you to ignore. All you have to do is find Pike. Kill him at your convenience. Nothing will come back to you as a result of his departure from the living."

Somewhat surprised by the thoroughness of his preparations, I said, "And exactly how much are you offering for this job?"

"I'll pay you two thousand dollars in gold—upon proof of Pike's untimely death."

"How do you expect me to prove I've dispatched the right man? You want me to bring his body back?"

"Return of the corpse isn't necessary. Pike wears a unique pair of solid silver spurs. Had 'em specially made in San Antone when we passed through. Murderous bastard won't turn 'em loose, 'less he was as dead as a beaver hat. Bring those spurs to me—and the money's yours."

"Got any idea where he went?"

"I know exactly where he is right this very minute. Worthless scum is drinking, whoring, and taking his leisure at the Blue Bottle Saloon, less than sixty miles from here in Coldwater. He and two of his friends arrived there over a week ago and haven't yet departed."

"How did you come by such information?"

"Friend of mine stopped over in Coldwater for a bit of fun and relaxation 'bout a week ago. Spotted Pike, Paxton Jefferies, and a three-fingered killer named Spider Clegg, having lunch together at a table in the front window of the Blue Bottle. I have no reason to believe they've left as yet. Near as I've been able to tell, Pike's making no effort to hide. Appears right proud of his killings. Has no worries about arrest or retaliation. My hope is that you'll bring about a change in his attitude."

"Mighty tough trio you've named off. I've only been in Dodge a short time, and have heard bloody tales about Pike's two friends ever since I hit town. Rumors going around would lead any reasonable man to some mighty apprehensive feelings about approaching Jefferies and Clegg."

"No doubt about it, Mr. Gault. They're a murderous, evil bunch. Personally have little doubt them boys are probably in league with Satan himself. Question is, will you take the job and do what I've asked?"

I thought Butcher's proposal over for about fifteen seconds. Stood at the bar, twirled my beaker of tarantula juice in a circle, and had to admit the proposition bore a number of fascinating aspects. Hell, at least half a dozen counties in Texas had warrants and posters out on me for a variety of murders. I'd killed the hell out of five thieving bastards in the Nations, and while only three other living men could testify to the event, all of Dodge still buzzed with the tale. Then, out of nowhere, Titus Butcher shows up and offers me a deputy sheriff's commission and badge. I'd be a lawman, for Christ's sake. The entire crazy-quilt state of affairs fired me up in a way I would never have believed possible.

Grabbed the badge and pile of paper from the bar and said, "I'm your man, Mr. Butcher."

Cowman's chin dropped to his chest. When his mist-filled eyes met mine again, he mumbled, "Thank you, sir. You'll never know how much I appreciate your decision."

"You'll appreciate it to the tune of a thousand dollars up front, with the rest payable when I return carrying Brady Pike's spurs."

Ole Titus didn't hesitate for a second. Dropped a heavy leather bag of gold double eagles on the bar, shook my hand, slapped me on the shoulder, and started to walk away. He turned and said, "I'm on the third floor. Room 303. Be looking forward to good news."

Next morning, I pinned on my shiny new badge, saddled up, and headed out on the sixty-mile ride to Coldwater.

When I arrived there, two days later, got the impression that the dusty Kansas town had all the appearance of an older, poorer, and more decrepit version of Dodge. Rough-cut board-and-batten buildings sprang from the rolling, grass-covered plains and, from a distance, presented the peculiar appearance of piles of buffalo bones bleaching in the sun. A single, dusty, near-deserted street passed through the jumbled collection of structures. Tied my animal to a hitch rack in front of the Blue Bottle Saloon and strolled inside.

Thick-necked, muscular, mustached bartender who sported a head that appeared to have survived an aborted scalping threw a ragged towel over his shoulder when I entered and said, "Welcome, first drink's on the house. What's your pleasure, sir?"

I ordered a better label of whiskey. He surprised me by

serving it up. Nervous man snatched several sneaky peeks at the badge on my chest as he poured the drink.

Took the first sip of his liquor before I asked, "Would you know a gent named Brady Pike on sight?"

He blinked like I'd slapped him, and hesitated before saying, "Mr. Pike and some of his friends arrived in town several weeks ago. They take lunch here every day. Usually sit at the table over by the window." He threw a nervous glance at the loud-ticking clock that hung on the wall over his back bar. Turned to me and said, "They should arrive in another hour or so."

I pointed to the table in the corner most distant from the entrance. In a voice that sounded colder than winter in the Dakotas, I said, "Would prefer you not announce my presence, or that I asked for Pike, when he enters. Soon as he and his compadres take their seats, want you to bring a clean glass to that table." He nodded. I took the bottle, ambled to the corner, and took a seat with my back to the wall.

Spent most of the next two hours watching half a dozen flies on the floor wrestle with a chunk of what looked like a piece of pig gristle, and trying my best to stay awake. Insect food war was interrupted a number of times by entering customers. One feller looked enough like a gunman to divert my attention from the wrestling bugs for quite a spell. But he took his liquor at the bar, and left as soon as he'd finished a single glass.

Just before one o'clock, I noticed a hand on top of the batwing doors. Two of the fingers had gone missing. Spider Clegg pushed his way inside and glanced around the room as though checking its contents for possible threat. He shoved his Boss of the Plains hat off, and let it hang down his back from a leather cinch strap. The double-row ammunition belt around his waist bristled with several pistols and knives. He mopped a sweaty brow, turned, and motioned to someone on the boardwalk.

A pair of equally heavily armed men stepped inside, and repeated the same cautious routine before sliding along the wall to the only table near the Blue Bottle's huge front window. I could hear the soft, musical jingle of well-made spurs as they took their seats.

The bartender flung the towel over his shoulder and sprinted to the gunmen's favorite eating spot when one of them motioned for him to approach. After a discussion I couldn't hear, he returned to the bar, got a clean glass, and headed for my table.

Whiskey slinger placed the tumbler near my bottle and whispered, "The feller facing the window is Brady Pike. Be careful of the man on his right. Pax Jefferies is a killer." Then he hoofed it to the back room to get whatever Pike and his friends had ordered to eat.

I'd already removed the badge. Had it stored in my vest pocket. Could tell, by what I had observed, that hiding the star was most probably a sound decision. Waited until food and a steaming pot of coffee were placed on their table before I stood. Pike poured three cups and sat the pot near his right hand. Slipped up near him and Clegg before any of them even realized they had company.

Jefferies saw me first. Alarmed, he jerked his gaze my direction as he said, "What the hell you want, you sneaky son of a bitch?"

Clegg's head snapped around. "Goddamn, Pike, I didn't even see him. Where'd you come from, mister?"

Pike dismissively glanced my way and sipped at his cup before he spoke. "Aw, hell, boys, don't think you need to worry none. This gent ain't gonna be a problem, are you, mister?"

My first shot went through the left side of Pike's head and splattered all manner of brain, bone, and blood in Jefferies's face. Poor gore-covered bastard was so shocked, I doubt he had time to think about the slug that punched a hole in his heart, blew through his spine, and lodged in the windowsill behind him, along with a gob of his insides.

A screaming Spider Clegg jumped out of his chair and hoofed it for the door. Blue whistler from my weak-side pistol hit him in back of the head. Knocked his flopping body to the boardwalk outside. I stepped to the door, glanced down, and discovered the bullet had departed through his mouth and taken most of his teeth with it. A gory pile of ivories lay on the bloody boards about a foot from where his head rested. He kept twitching like a dying rattlesnake, so I blasted him again. Got the sorry skunk behind the right ear that time. Second hole in ole Spider's already empty noggin stopped all that flopping around pretty damned quick.

Bent over the body, pulled Clegg's pistol, and dropped it in the bloody puddle near his hand. Quickly slipped back in the saloon and did the same with the other two as well. Placed Jefferies's pistol on the floor beside his chair, then wrapped Pike's still-warm fingers around the butt of his weapon, and laid it in his lap next to the coffee cup. Looked damned good when I finished.

Crazy-eyed bartender stormed to my side and appeared to go bug nutty. I couldn't understand a word he said for about a minute. Everything came out of his mouth in a jumble of incoherent phrases. A flurry of gestures seemed to make even less sense than what he said. 'Bout the time I got both my pistols reloaded, he managed to utter something understandable. "Jesus H. Christ, mister. You kilt all three of 'em so fast, I couldn't even see how you did it."

"Yeah, well, had to do 'em quick as I could. No need giving boys like these any kind of a chance. Might well have meant my death if I had. Started to shoot them from over in the corner, but felt I might miss from that distance. Had to get up close to do this job right."

He mopped at his brow with the bar rag. "But why? Why'd you kill 'em like that? Why not just arrest 'em and take 'em to jail?"

"I've been in jail. Didn't care for it. Don't think this crew would've liked it much either. They're a whole lot better off dead. So's the rest of the world." Stunned barkeep stumbled to the doors of his back room and disappeared.

Pike's head lolled on his neck stalk like a watermelon on a peach tree limb. Blood dripped from the hole I'd put in him, and collected in an ever-growing pool under his straight-backed chair. Grabbed his seat by one of its slats and pulled him away from the meal he'd not yet started. A half-full coffee cup dangled from his dead finger.

I snatched one of his booted feet up and dropped it on the table. Sure enough, he sported the most astonishing set of spurs on anybody in Kansas, or the world for all I knew. Sparkling rowels were as big around as two silver dollars. Best leatherwork I'd ever seen. Altogether, they were mighty impressive.

Once I'd retrieved everything needed to satisfy Titus Butcher's requirements, I headed for the door, only to be stopped by Coldwater's poor idiot of a town marshal. Silly son of a bitch didn't have any more sense about him than the near frantic bartender.

He gingerly stepped over Clegg's still-leaking carcass and said, "Good God Almighty. We ain't had this many killin's on a single day in more'n five years." He threw a sweaty glance at the bodies still sitting at the table. Ripped his hat off, and rubbed a shaking arm across his dripping face. "Sweet merciful heavens. Look at this mess." Then he turned puzzled eyes on me. "What in the blue-eyed hell's goin' on here, mister?"

By the time he got around to me, I'd put my badge back on and retrieved Butcher's warrant from my coat pocket. Handed the document to the astonished marshal, pointed at Pike's body, and said, "Dead man still trying to drink his coffee was wanted for the murder of a fifteen-year-old boy named Titus Butcher Junior. He balked at being arrested and taken back to Dodge for trial. Tried to pull on me. Found it necessary to kill him. Couldn't be avoided."

Coldwater's dazed marshal gaped at all the bodies again. "What about the other two?"

"Silly bastards attempted to aid their murderous friend. Piss-poor decision to draw on a man who's already armed and smoking." Reached over and placed a quieting hand on the marshal's still-quaking shoulder, smiled, and said, "Guess there just ain't no accounting for unbridled stupidity, is there?"

He shot the kind of look at me that implied I'd lost my mind. I reached down and snatched the warrant from his rubbery fingers. Folded it back up as I started for the door. Didn't get very far when he called out, "Where the hell you think you're goin', mister?"

Turned to see the man's once-nervous, agitated gaze had hardened dramatically. "Back to Dodge," I said.

His right hand came up on the grips of the pistol on his hip. "Not today, you ain't. There'll be a coroner's inquest quick as I can get everyone together. In the meantime, you'll have to sit in my jail till everything shakes out."

Pulled the papers out my pocket again and held them up for him to see. "You saw this warrant. That man was a cold-blooded murderer. He killed an unarmed boy. These other two attempted to aid him in my murder."

His grip tightened on the pistol butt. "All of that might well prove true, mister. But like I said, that's for the coroner's inquest to determine. Hell, anyone can show up wearin' a badge and claimin' whatever they want. But in my town, we'll wait for the coroner's findings just to make sure."

Now, I want what I'm about to say to be as crystal clear as a jug of stump-holler white lightning. I'd had no earthly intention of killing Coldwater's amazingly stupid town marshal when I arrived there. Didn't know the man, and wanted nothing more than to perform the job Titus Butcher had hired me to do and be on my way.

But when the law-bringing son of a bitch went to pull a pistol on me, I simply had no choice. Blasted the silly jackass into the next week before he could get his weapon leveled up on my guts. Big chunk of lead hit the stupid gomer dead center, and pitched him backward like a rag doll. He landed on top of the table where the rapidly cooling corpses of Pike and Jefferies still sat. Can't say as how

I actually *regretted* what he forced me to do. Except to
mention that his unexpected passing sure threw a kink in
my plans. Forced me into a run for my horse and a race
with a local posse back to Dodge.

Coldwater's irate citizens couldn't have been more'n
an hour or so behind when I hit town like I had a Fourth
of July whizbang tied to my ass. Hoofed it to Butcher's
room. Banged on his door. Wanted to pick up the rest of
my pay. Get the hell out of Dodge in a hurry.

When he finally let me in, and I dropped Brady Pike's
spurs on his bed, ole Titus wept like a baby. Shook my
hand so hard, I thought he'd rip my arm from its socket.
Didn't even have to ask for the money. He pressed another
sack of coins into my hand, and hugged me like a long-
lost son.

I quickly offered my thanks, said good-bye, and flew
back downstairs to my own room. Burst in unannounced
and found Trixie in *my* bed with a big hairy churnhead
who was going at her like a hard-rock miner finding his
first gold strike. God Almighty, but I've never been so
mad in my entire life. Couldn't believe she had nerve
enough to bring the big goober to *my* bed for cryin' out
loud. She'd never done it before. Leastways, if she had, I
didn't know about it.

Pea-brained, dim-witted fool didn't even bother to stop
what he was doing. Looked me straight in the eye and
said, "Gonna have to wait your turn, mister. Still got a
lotta riding left 'fore I head this bangtail to the stall."

Well, what he said got all over me like the smell of rotting meat on a July afternoon in West Texas. Stomped
over to the bed, grabbed the big dumb ox by the neck, and
jerked him off of Trixie's still-bouncing body. Got to admit, she was smarter than her customer. Death had accidentally found them both, and Trixie knew it. Agitated gal
jumped out of the bed buck-assed nekkid, and went to
running around the room screaming like the whistle on a
steam engine.

Reached out and grabbed her by the wrist as she raced

for the still-open door. Placed the muzzle of the pistol against her chest and pulled the trigger. Dirty-legged whore hit the floor like a sack of bricks.

Gal's last customer crawled under the bed. I fired all four of the remaining rounds into the mattress. Wasn't sure I hit him, but I was in too big a hurry to find out. Grabbed as much in the way of food, clothing, and other valuables as could be had, and hoofed it for the street.

Fogged out of town and headed south as fast as good horseflesh could travel. No doubt existed in my mind I was followed, because killing a woman, even one of astonishingly low repute, tended to be frowned on just about everywhere.

Jayhawkin' sons of bitches almost caught up with me a few miles north of the Canadian. But I headed east, and hid for several days in Red Rock Canyon. Good water and shelter available there, plus plenty of places to fort up should my pursuers have found me. Guess none of them bastards had ever even seen or heard of the place, thank God. Started running again soon as it felt safe. For the next three weeks, I rode, ran on foot beside my animal, walked uncountable miles, and hardly slept a wink.

At times, me and the horse kept moving for eighteen hours at a stretch. Had damned little to eat—mostly what I could steal from any farm or ranch that presented itself along the way. Trip was particularly hard on Fuzzy, my mount, but it had to be done. And all glory be to the Man Upstairs because once we made it into the safety of Texas, them Kansas lawdogs finally gave up the chase.

Slipped into Fort Worth, and got myself completely reoutfitted and resupplied before kicking for points farther south. Didn't stop running till I got to Uvalde. Along the way, I promised God that if he let me survive my escapades in Dodge, I'd try my best to behave. Sometimes, it's damned hard to keep a promise. Especially those we make to the Man Upstairs.

16

"Beautiful, ain't it, Moon?"

Couldn't believe my luck. Stopped at the first cow country oasis I came upon in Uvalde. Rugged back-country watering hole had a weathered plank sign over the door that looked a hundred years old. Flame-burned lettering dubbed the saloon the EL PERRO BLANCO CANTINA.

Picked up a bottle at the bar and headed for the farthest corner. Good God, but I was as dry as the bleached bones of a year-dead longhorn lying in the wastelands of the Big Bend country. My trail-tender behind hadn't hit the chair good when I overheard a hatchet-faced feller at the table next to mine trying his best to rent a small horse ranch to a less-than-interested leather pounder. In spite of a more-than-reasonable-sounding offer, his cowboy customer appeared so broke, he couldn't have changed his mind or paid attention. Discussion got so heated, the frustrated brush popper abruptly pushed his chair away from the table. Wooden legs squealed against rough-cut flooring, and he angrily stomped out.

Sounded like a good opportunity to me. And being as how my suit coat, wallet, and saddlebags probably contained more money than anyone within a hundred miles had seen in years, I leaned over and said, "If he's not interested, mister, I am. Been looking for a small spread to settle on for sometime now. Willing to pay you whatever the asking price is, so long as we can work up some kind of mutually acceptable plan whereby my rental payments can be applied to a future purchase."

My God, you'd have thought I magically grew wings, a halo, and floated down from Heaven on a golden cloud. Gaunt gent jumped out of his chair, grabbed my hand, and damn near shook it off. "Name's Justin Farnsworth, sir. I can assure you beyond any doubt whatever that we can work out a deal. Hell, I'll even let you draw up the agreement. Word it any way you like. We'll take it to my lawyer, Mr. Arnette Dagget, and have him notarize the deal. You can move in at your earliest possible convenience."

"How many acres we talking about, Mr. Farnsworth?"

The stringy rancher rolled himself a smoke, lit up, took a puff, and said, "More than enough to start you on the way to a working horse operation. Guarantee you'll love the place."

"Would I have to do any building and such?"

"No, sir, not a bit. Property has an existing ranch house, fine barn, and a split-rail corral large enough for at least thirty head. Now, I'll admit the accommodations are a bit on the rough side, but they should prove more than adequate for a start."

"I gather someone did a lot of work."

"Feller who recently vacated the property leased this acreage from me for more'n ten years. Poor son of a bitch knew about as much about raisin' horses as I do about building steam engines. Should have knowed better when he arrived here from New by-God York."

Well, that was something of a surprise. Said, "You rented land to a greenhorn from New York?"

His nose scrunched and he looked a bit too sly for a second or so. "Said he'd raised horses afore somewheres in the green and grassy areas in the northern part of that fine Yankee state. 'Course, I'll have to admit, that's a damned long way from the rough and tumble of workin' with the bangtails here in South Texas."

"Couldn't make a go, I take it?"

"No, sir, he couldn't. Man just never was able to adjust. His wife and young 'uns had it even tougher. Felt right sorry for them kids of his. On top of everything else, I had to make downward alterations in his rent every year, till he finally went bust. Guess he's back home in upstate New York by now. Son of a bitch snuck off. Left me holdin' the bag on a whole year's worth of back rent."

Sipped from my glass, then said, "Sure would like to take a look at the place before I sign any papers or give up any money."

Sounded like a carnival barker when he said, "Oh, hell, yes. Understand completely. As you can see, I ain't busy at this very moment, and can take you out to the ranch right now if you'd like." Slapped me on the back like a long-lost brother when I stood, and away we went.

Farnsworth led me more than an hour west, almost to the Nueces River. Country was wild, rough, and desolate. Steep, rocky arroyos covered with tangled brush sliced down to a shallow, slow-moving creek not far from the coarse ranch house. Some of the water-carved gullies were so uneven, you couldn't cross them for long stretches. No doubt in my mind that the creek eventually found its way to the Nueces.

Can't say it surprised me in the least that a native New Yorker would have trouble making a success of it in such a rough and untamed spot. But, hell, couldn't condemn the man much, because I wasn't a rancher either—simply needed a place to lay low.

We reined up on the east side of the creek. I sat on Fuzzy and let him drink. Turned to the property's owner and said, "I'll take it."

Farnsworth smiled like I'd saved him from the fiery pit. He said, "Damned glad to hear it, sir. Oh, didn't get your name."

"Moon. Henry Moon. And I do require one thing, Mr. Farnsworth. Privacy. The ranch seems to afford me plenty, being as how it's so far from town and all. But I must insist on being left to myself. My visits to Uvalde will be limited—perhaps only to attend an occasional worship service, or resupply when necessary."

"No need to worry, Mr. Moon. Your closest neighbor is a Mexican family. Juan Martinez and his brood have a hacienda about five miles north and west of here. Doubt you'll see any of them folks more'n two or three times a year."

"Noticed a storefront church when I arrived."

"Yes indeed. The Reverend Nathanial Hobbs runs the Baptist version of the come-to-Jesus business in these parts. He arrived in town two years ago. Our congregation has only recently begun construction on a real honest-to-goodness church building. Hobbs preaches out of what once served as an express office a few doors down from the saloon. Sure he'll be pleased to have you attend."

"And law. What about that?"

"Reverend Hobbs sees to our souls. Town Marshal Hector Stamps sees to the habits that land us outside Mr. Hobbs's purview. Hector's getting on up there in years, but we don't need much in the way of law here in Uvalde anyhow. Right tame. You're gonna love how peaceful it is around these parts, Mr. Moon."

By nightfall, we'd visited lawyer Arnette Dagget's office and drawn up an agreement that was more than generous in my direction. When I dropped two years advance rent on the property in his lap, thought Farnsworth would weep.

Next morning, I purchased a spring wagon, and bought everything I could lay my hands on at the local mercantile. Store was run by a cheerful, ruddy-cheeked feller named Lorenzo Jacks who appeared to have never met a meal he didn't like. He even gave me a first-timer's ten-percent discount on everything I bought. Leastways, he claimed he did.

I spent the next few months putting my newly acquired house back in order. After the previous occupants of the dwelling had left, several varieties of varmints had moved in. Worst of it was the snakes and scorpions. Found a rattler as big around as my arm under the bed. Scared up a long-handled hoe out near the corral, and chopped his big ole head off. Became real careful about flinging my feet to the floor every morning upon waking after that unnerving discovery. Got to where I took a long hard look all around the room before getting out of the bed from then on. Harbored no hankering for a fate like that poor drover of Mr. Bloodsworth's.

The former residents had departed in such a rush, they'd left most of their furnishings. Covered with a thick layer of dust, those fixtures would never have been thought of as the best money could buy, but they served me well enough.

I especially favored the Excelsior cook stove kept under a lean-to shed attached to the end of the house farthest from the sleeping area. Couldn't find a spot of rust on its beautifully forged body. Cast-iron beast came all the way from Quincy, Illinois. Looked brand-new. Couldn't imagine why anyone went to such an expense. Most times, the weather was so hot I was reluctant to fire it up. But I still liked the thing anyway.

Attended the Reverend Hobbs's church twice during that first month. Sat on the back pew. Had totally forgotten how much I missed the company of good people, heartfelt music, and the presence of a forgiving Lord.

Second time I showed for the whooping, hollering, preaching, and singing, spotted a damned nice-looking gal a few pews closer to the front. Tall, rangy, and auburn-haired. Her chiseled good looks made her something akin to tomboyish in appearance. Really liked the way her short-cropped hair curled around her ear. The curve of her neck lit me up like a Roman candle.

Did some discreet inquiries, and discovered she was the only daughter of my landlord, the peerless Mr. Farnsworth. Don't know why, but he wasn't in attendance on the days I spent eyeballing her every chance I got.

The talkative Mr. Jacks said, "Her name's Ella. She's a fine young woman, but headstrong as hell. I've heard as how she's tomboy enough to have beat the hell out of most of the young men in these parts at one time or 'tother. Most of 'em figure she'd make a right fine catch bein' as how her father's the richest man in these parts. Yeah, Ella's 'bout as beautiful as they come, but rough as a cob."

Next time I showed for services, caught her sneaking glances my direction. Stopped Farnsworth on the board-walk outside the church and kept him talking, until the girl presented herself. He introduced us. Could tell right off she was way more than a little bit interested in Henry Moon, and a lot better-looking the closer I got. Gal had sky blue eyes and the kind of mouth that could make a man think less-than-pure thoughts.

Way she batted those big blues at me left not a single doubt in my mind as to her intentions. It's like that with small-town girls. Local boys get all the new wore off of them quicker than double-greased lightning. Stranger comes along, and a whole new world opens up for such love-starved females. Leastways, that's what I always thought, and told myself, at every lustful opportunity.

Next morning, Ella Farnsworth reined up outside my front doorway before daylight hit. Woke me from a dreamy sleep when she fired off a pistol. Grabbed my own smoke pole and jerked the door open. Came damned close to shooting her off that pinto pony she rode. But I have to admit, I wasn't a bit surprised by her fiery appearance. Fact is, I expected her.

Gal still held the smoking gun when she crossed her

arms over the saddle horn and said, "Get dressed, Mr. Moon."

"What the hell for?" I mumbled through the haze of unfinished repose.

"Sun's comin' up in a bit."

"Usually happens every morning, if I remember correctly, Miss Farnsworth. Could be wrong about such definitive statements, though, seeing as how, most mornings, I sleep until good daylight wakes me up."

"Well, you're already up now, Moon. No time to waste. So put your pants on. We're going for a ride."

I figured what the hell. Might as well go along. Didn't have anything to lose, and not much else to do. Like most men, I got to thinking—and hoping. Told myself it could be she had something special in mind. Something real special.

I couldn't have been more wrong about her purpose. She led me out to what had to be the tallest pile of rocks within fifty miles. We tied our animals to a mesquite tree at the base, and started our climb to the top along a narrow, steep, but well-worn trail.

As I struggled along behind her, she said, "Ain't as high as Turkey Mountain. Don't even have an official name as far as I know." She stopped just long enough to point out a barely visible rock formation ahead. "Been callin' this spot Elephant Butte ever since I was ten years old." In the rapidly diminishing shadows, the stack of stones truly did look something like an elephant. "There's a fine view of your place from up here, too, Mr. Moon. 'Course we won't be able to see it till good light."

By the time we arrived at the peak, I huffed and puffed like a fully loaded M.K. & T. freight trying to get started on oil-slicked rails. We hadn't managed to settle ourselves more than a minute or so when she handed me a bacon and egg sandwich. I was hungry as hell and appreciated her good sense. 'Bout then, a glorious sun peeked over the horizon and introduced a barren but wildly beautiful world to a whole new day.

Soft, amber glow crept across a desolate land in vivid
hues that started with purple, turned to blue, then brown
and orange, with hints of almost every color of the rain-
bow. Remember thinking, it's breathtaking and decep-
tively peaceful.

Ella sounded captivated when she breathed, "Beautiful,
ain't it, Moon?"

Tried, but couldn't remember a point in years when I'd
had either the time or inclination to stop and appreciate
anything like a sunrise. Been running and killing ever
since I broke the chains that held me to my abusive, lunatic father. The realization of how barren the lonely life I'd
lived up till then was hit me like the entirety of Elephant
Butte had fallen on me. Felt as though God dropped an
anvil on my heart, all the way from Heaven's front gate.

Only thing I could choke out was, "Yes, Ella, as you
say. It's absolutely beautiful."

Thought the gal was still engrossed in the event, because she didn't turn my way when she said, "I've never
brought anyone else to this spot before, Moon. This is a
very private place for me. I love my time here, mainly
because I can't remember anyone else showing up to
bother me. Never thought the boys here'bouts would appreciate just sitting and watching the sun come up. I knew
you would as soon as Pa introduced us yesterday." Then
she grabbed my hand and said, "I could feel it when you
touched me."

That act of unpracticed tenderness, shown by a girl
who'd been described to me as wilder than an uncurried
fuzztail, came as a complete surprise. Like just about
every other woman-hungry man in the world, I thought
for sure her aim that glorious morning was to see how fast
she could get me out of my pants and into hers.

But as time passed, and we marveled together at the
waking of the world, I came to realize that Ella Farnsworth obviously lived with the burden of a misleading
reputation. To put it bluntly, she was lonely. About as
lonely as anyone I'd ever met.

Although the morning light revealed hints of a hardened personality etched in the fine lines of her young face, I quickly determined those marks were most likely the result of the only defenses available for a very private person forced to lead a public life as the solitary child of Uvalde's richest man. For those reasons, and others, I felt an immediate kinship and affection for the girl.

From that morning forward, till it got so hot even Satan would've hunted for some shade, Ella came by every other day or so, and we headed for Elephant Butte to watch God bring the world back to life. Beautiful girl kissed me for the first time up there. Sweetest, most invigorating contact I'd ever had with any female—well, maybe with the exception of Charlotte Hickerson. Difference was that Charlotte gave up everything quick as she could. Ella offered ruby lips and the burning *possibility* of mysterious things yet to come. Been my experience that, when it comes to women, mystery wins every time.

But Elephant Butte wasn't that gal's only surprise. After about three weeks of our early morning raids into the wilds for her sunrise ceremonies, she showed up extra early on one particularly beautiful daybreak. Carried several cane poles and a can of worms.

"What's all this?" I asked.

"Don't know if Pa showed you or not, but there's a stock tank about two miles northeast of here. Actually, it's on the land you leased. Has some mighty good pan-sized fish. We're going fishin', Moon."

Couldn't believe my ears. Ella liked fishing. What more could a man want? Hell, she was beautiful, rode like a wild Indian, brought out the most romantic kinds of feelings in me, and best of all, we enjoyed each other's company.

I spent that morning lying on the edge of the pond, under the shade of a crab apple tree, watching my cork bob around and sneaking glances at Ella. Horses grazed in the tall grass. Glorious sun peeked between thin clouds. God

Almighty, pretty sure I felt better than I had at any other time of my life.

As the months passed, gossips from church spread the news around town that we were an item. Suppose most such talk got going because we started sitting together during church services. Even a half-blind schoolteacher could have spotted our infatuation with one another.

Six or eight weeks after we met, Ella helped me buy some ponies from a local dealer who often did business with her father. Girl knew more about horses than most men. I needed the animals to keep up the impression of a greenhorn rancher intent on going into the horse-raising business. 'Course, I only purchased enough to maintain the image. No one seemed to notice, or care, that my herd never amounted to anything like what a man needed to keep himself going in a real honest-to-God ranching concern.

My life appeared to have come around to something like boring normality. And, I have to admit, everything was going so good, I couldn't wait to get up in the morning and see what the day brought—especially if it had anything to do with beautiful Ella. She surprised and amazed me in some fashion almost every day.

Got to the point where everything was so satisfying, I only felt it necessary to carry one pistol. Such a realization was something of a milestone for me. For the first time since the life-changing folly of *La Honda*, I felt at peace with myself and the direction my tumultuous existence appeared to be headed. Days, and even weeks, went by where I enjoyed myself on a level I'd never experienced before, and somehow felt I had no right to expect.

And then, from the dusty trails leading north to Kansas, an arrogant son of a bitch named Bruno Kleitz showed up. May as well have been Satan himself. Now that I think on it, there's a real possibility he was the devil. Anyway, didn't take long after his appearance before everything in my almost picture-perfect new world went straight to hell on a bobsled.

17

"We don't want any trouble."

I'd never so much as heard the name Bruno Kleitz mentioned by anyone of my acquaintance in Uvalde, until the big joker burst through the door of El Perro Blanco late one scorching afternoon. Justin Farnsworth and I were engaged in a friendly attempt to enjoy a pleasant, and uneventful, drink at the time.

Happened to glance over my landlord's shoulder and see a great hulking beast of a feller fling the batwing doors open and stomp to the middle of the room. Could tell from the vein pooched out and throbbing against his temple that, whoever he was, the sweet light of good fellowship and happiness had not existed in his life for some time.

Creature pointed a finger the size of the handle on a ball-peen hammer at me, shook all over like he might collapse from anger, and yelped, "Done heard 'bout you, Moon. Close friends done tole me everything. You're a woman-stealin' son of a bitch."

Leaned toward Farnsworth and said, "Who the hell is this amazingly tall stack of cow shit?"

Big man didn't hear me, and kept up with his tirade. "Good God, but a man can't even leave town on a tiny-assed cattle drive 'thout some bastard like you showin' up and causin' trouble, Moon. Done got it in my mind as how, before this situation resolves itself completely out, I'll probably have to kill you deader'n a busted hoe handle."

Justin didn't bother to answer me, but twirled around in his chair. "What the hell are you doin', Bruno? Have you completely lost what little mind you ever had? Get the hell outta here and go on about your business."

Sounded like a Mississippi cotton farmer when Bruno shot back, "Don't mean any offense, but you can shut the hell up, Mr. Farnsworth. This ugly gob of spit ain't gonna come to my hometown, set hisself up as some kind of respected rancher, and get away with stealin' the one and only love of my life."

Farnsworth chuckled under his breath. "Ella's a lot of things, Bruno. She ain't the love of anybody's life—and most especially yours."

"The hell you say. Bet I breathed in most of the topsoil between Uvalde and Dodge on' at 'ere cattle drive to Kansas so's I could git back home with some money in my pocket and marry my beloved. Done tole her what was what before I left. Done tole her we'd git married when I got back. Settle down. Maybe have a house full of kids."

Farnsworth stood and held up a peacemaking hand. "Don't know what you've been drinkin', Bruno, but that's the biggest load of total bull feathers I've heard in years. Far as I'm able to determine, my daughter ain't no one's beloved, and she ain't about to marry anybody. Why don't you go on back to your father's place and cool off, or sober up—whichever works best. We don't want any trouble."

Justin's entreaty had absolutely no effect on the blond-haired giant. Bruno shook his finger with considerably more force, and yelled even louder when he said, "Damned if'n I will. Wasn't gone but six or eight months

at the most, for Christ's sake. Thought that whole time
my Ella wuz a-waitin' fer me. Come home and find out
this hymn-singing, dandified weasel done went and stole
my gal."

A blind man could tell Farnsworth was on the verge of
busting a major blood vessel in his own head. He almost
shouted, "Ella never consented to your proposals of mar-
riage, Bruno, and you know it. Far as I'm aware, she could
barely stand the sight of you. And you know why. Hell's
bells, boy, damn near everyone in town knows what you
did to her."

My landlord had finally got the fearsome Bruno's attention with that one. The brute snapped, "That's a damnable lie. When I left for Dodge, we had planned to tie the
knot when I got back. Ella loved me, and I loved her. This
here sweet-talkin' bastard showed his ugly face, turned
her head, and filled her soul with deceitful lies. He's done
went and flipped my whole life over on its back like a
stranded armadiller. Bewitched my beautiful Ella. Re-
made her into a heartless, hateful witch. Ain't gonna have
it. Gonna kill 'im, and worry about the consequences
later."

I'd heard enough. Hell, more than enough. Slowly got
to my feet, eased Farnsworth to one side, and pulled my
jacket away from the pistol resting across my belly.
"We've never met, but you don't appear to be anything
like an accomplished gunman to me, Mr. Kleitz."

"I can hold my own with egg-sucking dogs like you."

"Seriously doubt that. You don't have the least idea the
kind of tiger you've grabbed onto. But if you plan to kill
somebody, you'd best get at it right now. Just know this.
You so much as twitch a finger toward that smoke pole on
your lardy hip, and I'll put so many holes in your sorry
hide, me and Mr. Farnsworth will be able to read tomorrow's San Antonio newspaper through them."

For the first time, I got a good look at his eyes. They
were the color of dog piss. God had gifted ole Bruno with
mad-looking yellow orbs like some kind of giant, poison-

ous lizard. They blinked real fast, and almost crossed, always a good sign from a man you just might have to kill. Think it surprised Kleitz that I'd stood up to him. Now I had the stupid lunkhead thinking about the possibility of dying in a pistol fight. Leastways, hoped I did. Hard to tell with a man who looks like he has all the brains of an empty water trough.

Bruno tried to recover, and went to shaking his finger at me again. "Guess you must think you're some kind of gunhand, Moon. Big-talkin', no-doin' sons of bitches like you don't scare me one damned bit."

He had to strain to hear me when I said, "You should be afraid, Bruno, very afraid. Death is looking you right in the face. You should be shaking right down to the soles of those canoes covering your feet."

My little joke went right over his anvil-thick head. Watched him try to reason out what I'd said. He looked like a redbone hound locked in a futile attempt to read one of Shakespeare's plays, or perhaps reason out the chemical properties of homemade liquor.

After some seconds of what appeared to be painful thought, Kleitz whipped his shaking finger at me again and blubbered, "We'll take this disagreement up another time, you thievin' bastard. Best keep on the lookout for me, Moon. First chance I git, gonna bust you open like a ripe melon, stomp a ditch in you, and then stomp 'er dry." He cackled at his own effort at humor, and headed for the door. Hit the batwing so hard, thought for a second he'd knocked it off the brass hinges.

Once I'd made certain the creature had truly vacated the premises, returned to my table with Farnsworth and said, "Is he truly dangerous, or simply a mouthy blow-hard?"

"Oh, he's dangerous for damned sure. Not prone to making idle threats either. Over a four- or five-year span, think Bruno's beaten or stomped the juice out of almost every man and boy around here that he believed had so much as glanced at Ella."

"Why in the hell didn't anyone warn me about him?"

"We all thought the poor, stupid critter left town for good. That tale he told about how much Ella loved him is the biggest pile of cow flops I've ever heard. Reason he struck out on the drive in the first place was because she'd made it crystal clear just how little affection actually existed between them."

Took a sip from my beaker of tonsil paint and leaned back in my chair. "Well, I'd prefer not to have any trouble with the blithering idiot if possible. But I won't run, and won't let him do me, or Ella, any harm. Best inform Mr. Bruno Kleitz and his family that should he do anything to threaten our health, I'll kill him graveyard dead quicker than a newborn can get the hiccups."

Nothing I'd learned about Justin Farnsworth led me to believe he was a man given to a healthy load of stupid. Way he looked at me when I said what I did indicated he believed every word that came out of my mouth. And I have full faith he took my message to the astonishingly witless Bruno and his kinfolk. But telling a man as pea-brained as Kleitz anything is, most of the time, about as useful as speaking Mandarin to a tree full of squirrels.

Next time I saw Ella, she said, "Don't worry about the big dumb ox. He's all talk."

"Not according to what I've heard. Way I understand past events, ole Bruno has proved quite a thorn in your beautiful paw over the past few years."

Her chin dropped to her chest, and she shook her head like a weary animal. "True enough. Had more'n my share of problems with him. Guess the worst was when he beat the bejabbers out of Tony Madigan for sparkin' me some."

"What do you mean by 'bejabbers'?"

"Bruno snuck up behind Tony one night out in front of the El Perro Blanco. Jumped on the boy and gave him one helluva thrashin'. Doc said Bruno broke every bone in Tony's face. Took that poor busted-up boy almost a year to recover. He was one good-looking kid. Leastways, up until Bruno got through whompin' on him. Poor Tony left town soon as he could ride. Never came back. And there was one other thing, too."

"What?"

"He tried to force himself on me about every other day for longer than I'd like to remember. Ripped most of my clothes off at least twice a month. I fought him off most times, and that's not an easy thing to do. Thought he might be on the verge of doin' me in the last time he jumped on me. Pa's threatened to kill him if he didn't straighten up. Might as well have been talking to a mesquite bush. Unfortunately, Bruno's always done as he pleased."

Damn, but her revelation of that monster's past sins hit me like a load of bricks. Made my feelings on the matter as unmistakable as possible when I said, "Told your father I'd kill Mr. Bruno Kleitz deader than hell in a parson's front parlor myself if he made any move to hurt either of us. I meant every word of it, Ella."

She held my hand, flashed me a tender smile, and said, "I know, but don't worry, Henry. Nothing's gonna happen." Suffice it to say, Ella Farnsworth would never be able to make a living as a fortune-teller with a traveling carnival.

I noticed that her former beau started shadowing us not long after our little dustup in the saloon. Spotted him one morning trailing along behind when we went out to Elephant Butte. Got to where every Sunday, the smug bastard sat in the pew right behind us during the worship services. Couple of times he followed me over to the Farnsworth hacienda when Ella invited me over for supper. And while he never did anything out of the way, or even popped off at the mouth again, his behavior got me madder than the buzzard that circled a sick heifer for three hours before it realized the cow was only asleep.

Came a point where Kleitz's behavior bordered on the creepy. For a man who couldn't pour rainwater out of a mule-eared boot, 'less the instructions were printed on the heel, he possessed an uncanny ability to show up no matter where I decided to go. Can't count on all my fingers the times he appeared like a materializing ghost at the cantina within a minute of my arrival. Same thing happened to Ella. Girl got mighty agitated after about two months of such conduct on his part.

She rode over to my place late one afternoon, so we could sit on my front porch and watch the sun go down. Noticed, for the first time since we met, she carried a Remington pistol on her hip. No teensy-weensy little female-type pocket popper either.

Pointed at the weapon and said, "Now that's new and different. When did you start packin'? Thought all those warlike Comanches lived up in the Nations now."

Her eyes dropped and she toed around at a rough spot on one of the planks under her foot. "Don't get mad, Henry, but Bruno scared me."

That one stood me up in a hurry. Grabbed her by the shoulders. "What do you mean by scared you? What the hell did he do?"

"Aw, nothin' really."

Gently shook the girl, then used my finger to tilt her head up so I could see her eyes. "If that's the case, Ella, you wouldn't be carrying a gun right now. So tell me what he did."

She turned away and talked to the dying sun. "He caught me 'bout dark yesterday on the boardwalk in town. Jerked me into an alley and ran his hand down the front of my pants. We rassled around for a bit. But he dragged me down, and pretty much took advantage of me. Not altogether, but he sure tried."

"I'll just be damned."

"He's as strong as an ox, and it took some doin', but I finally got away from him like I'd done before. Think he might have just let me go on purpose. Big jackass laughed at me when I ran away. Guess he'd got what he always wanted. Still and all, he tore my pants to ribbons and ripped my shirt open. Don't know how I got back home and nobody managed to see me in such a terrible state."

I jumped off the porch and headed for the corral. Ella ran along behind and grabbed me by the arm. "What are you gonna do, Henry?"

"Time has come for Bruno Kleitz to meet his Maker. I'll find the soulless son of a bitch, then kill him."

She latched onto my arm and went to begging. "Let it go, Moon. Nothin' he did is worth the possibility of you dyin' over it. Besides, you're new here and don't know how powerful Bruno's family is. He could do whatever he wanted with me and then kill both of us. His family would buy him out of it."

Couldn't believe she didn't want any action taken against the bastard for his obviously brutal behavior. Grabbed her by the shoulders again and said, "No man should ever be allowed to so much as touch a woman if she doesn't want it. What Kleitz did went way beyond an unwanted touch. There's graveyards full of bastards like him who did less, and got sent to Jesus by men just like me."

Tears streamed down her cheeks. "But if you kill him, people will find out what happened to me." She turned away. "I don't want anyone in town to be aware of it. It's bad enough knowing that he felt like he could do what he did and get away with the act." A pall of resignation dropped over her face. "Actually, I'm surprised something like this hasn't happened before now. It's not like he hasn't made previous attempts. I've just always let his brutal advances pass. If you confront him, your actions could get us all killed."

Well, hard as it was, I let Bruno's violent act pass for Ella's sake. That single errant decision was perhaps one of the worst I ever made. Secretly promised myself that if anything else wayward occurred, the stupid son of a bitch wouldn't see the next morning's light. Should've gone ahead and shot hell out of the worthless slug that afternoon.

One of my old friend Cutter Sharpe's favorite sayings kept ringing in my ears. He used to light up, go into something of a philosophical trance, and say, "Eli, you should never put off killing any man who needs killing right now. Simple way of thinking I've always lived by. Will serve you well to adopt the same attitude. Failure might cause you to wake up shoveling coal in Hell."

Jesus, man should've been writing books.

18

---•◆•---

"Can't let wolves eat him, Moon."

Next evening, I saddled up and moseyed over to the Farnsworth place for a weekly dinner with Ella and her father that she got me started on right after we met. She skillfully hid her feelings from Justin, but I could still see the impact of the previous day's events in her eyes. Felt right sorry for her, and angry beyond words that I hadn't gone ahead and rubbed the "Bruno" problem out of her life like wiping crumbs off the supper table.

By the time we'd finished a fine meal, the deepening twilight made it difficult to see from the lamp-lit safety of their home into the darkness outside. I stepped onto the front porch to have a smoke. Got the first puff down, and there was a rush of movement in the darkness. Barely saw Bruno's cannonball-sized fist coming at my head in time to dodge most of the blow. Couple of his knuckles glanced off the side of my surprised noggin just above the ear. Felt like I'd been hit with a hatchet. The jolt split my scalp, and sticky blood flooded into my ear and mouth.

He laughed and barked, "I'm gonna have fun kickin' the dog crap outta you, Moon."

I staggered about two steps, went down like a felled oak, and landed on my face next to a woodpile Justin kept on the porch for easy access during the winter. Thank God I had enough presence of mind still available to immediately roll to one side. Thought I heard Ella scream as I scrambled around on the dirty porch. Her father hollered as well. Sounded like all the shouting, tumult, and commotion came from somewhere underwater, though.

Bruno's second lick whistled past an ear that rang like cathedral bells, and crashed through the inch-thick planks of their porch beside my head like a ten-pound sledgehammer. Splintering lumber and dust filled the evening air. I tried an evasive move in the opposite direction, and almost fell off the porch.

Stumbled to my less-than-helpful feet, staggered to one of the props holding the veranda's roof up, and in vain, slapped my side for the pistol I'd left hanging on a peg inside the doorway. By that point, my eyes had finally adjusted to the dying light. Glanced up to see Kleitz down on his knees trying to pull his hand out of the shattered mess he'd made. Had no idea how the big goober got stuck, but he went to bellowing like a wounded bull, and jerked a sizable stack of boards loose before he ripped free.

Foot-long piece of rough-cut timber was stuck to his hand by a tenpenny nail that went through the palm and protruded from the other side. He swayed to his feet, grabbed the board with his free hand, whimpered like a hurt child, and ripped the kindling from his injured fist. Stream of blood shot from the wound and spurted two feet my direction.

He squeezed his hand and yelped, "Damn you, Moon. You're gonna pay heavy for this."

Saw Ella jump on the thug's back and claw at his face. He brushed her away like she was nothing more than a nuisance fly. Her father grabbed at one of the gorilla's arms, and called for him to give up the fight. Big man smacked Justin between the eyes with a hellish lick. Watched as the poor man dropped like a gunnysack full of rocks.

A guttural grunt escaped Kleitz's heaving chest. He turned and charged my direction again. Shook my fogged-up brain box, dance-stepped out of his way, and watched as he went through the 4×4 wooden roof prop like it was a matchstick. Big bastard lost his balance when the support snapped. He half staggered, half fell into the darkness, and went headfirst into the trunk of an ancient live oak a few feet from the house. Heard what I thought were neck bones cracking. Leastways, that's what I hoped the sound was.

Took a couple of steps his direction to check on what I felt sure would be a dead body. Damned if the loutish swine didn't stand, shake his bloodied head, and make another run at me. Tried to get out of the way, but he swooped in with both arms open, grabbed me up like a bear capturing prey, and started to squeeze the life right out of me. As he swung his head back and forth, hairy chunks of gore from the scalp wound splattered all over me. Crushing muscles like iron bands tightened huge arms 'round my waist, and the air whooshed out of crushed lungs so fast I couldn't believe it.

Used my open palms to slap him upside his ears. Popping him didn't appear to faze the crazed beast in the least. Butted his nose with my forehead as hard as I could. Cartilage snapped like a piece of rotten cottonwood branch and punched a sizable hole through the skin. Got a mouthful of his blood as it spewed into my face. Crushing grip around my waist tightened. Little more pressure, and my ribs would've snapped.

Everything around us started to fade. Figured I only had one more thing to try before he killed me. Placed a blood-saturated palm on his cheek. Twisted his head sideways, slid my thumb into the corner of his eye, and gouged the eyeball out. Ugly yellow sucker made a right strange popping sound when it dropped onto his cheek.

Big son of a bitch let go of me pretty damned quick, and screamed so loud I can't imagine how people in Uvalde didn't hear him. Then he went to puking. Sprayed the stuff all over me, the porch, woodpile, everything within ten feet around. God Almighty, but the man must have eaten a gallon of bunkhouse chili for lunch that day.

Next thing I knew, he stood in front of me and held his eyeball up to the side of his head like he was trying to still see with the poor damaged glob. From God only knows where, he'd also managed to grab up an ax. Jesus, but the scene would've made one hell of a picture. Both of us stared at each other like madmen. Bruno held his eyeball in one hand, the ax in his other. He moved the dislocated orb back and forth in his fingers, and cried like a little kid.

He advanced on me again, swung the ax several times, but to no effect. Vision from his good eye was blocked by blood freely flowing from the wound on top of his head. Didn't slow him down much, though. He started across the porch, stepped into the hole he'd made when he swung at me the first time, and fell to his knees. The ax slipped from his blood- and puke-slicked hand, flew sideways, and stuck in the wall.

I figured the whole mess had run its course. But through willpower impossible for me to comprehend, the big brute managed to bring himself upright and stand. Heard something beside my ear, and half turned in time to see Ella's pistol-filled hand appear. Big blaster went off less than two feet from my face.

Bruno groaned, staggered a step backward, recovered, and lurched our way once more. He still held the gory eyeball like it was a coal miner's lamp guiding him to the object of an undying wrath. Second slug she sent his way punched a hole in his right cheek. Third one hit him in the throat. He made a nasty gurgling, retching sound, dropped the yellow eyeball, and grabbed at his neck. Have to admit, the girl was a damned good shot.

Shot giant made unspeakable air-sucking noises and

sagged like a hundred-pound sack of feed grain with a hole cut in the bottom corner. Ella dropped the pistol, and ran to help her father. Thank God, the blow he'd suffered didn't do much more than raise an egg-sized knot right between his eyes. Once we'd got Justin on his feet again, the three of us stood over Kleitz's limp body for almost a minute and didn't say anything. Still believe that all three of us felt certain he'd probably try to get up again. For a spell, that Texas evening got as quiet as an open grave at midnight.

Ella finally broke the silence. "What the hell are we gonna do now?"

Farnsworth waved at the mess on his front porch like a man bewildered. "We'll have to get Hector Stamps out here. Tell him what happened."

Thought about that for a minute before I said, "You can't tell anyone that Ella fired the shots that killed Kleitz."

At the same time father and daughter said, "Why not?"

"Because everyone within fifty miles of Uvalde knows Bruno and Ella's history. First thing that's going to happen out of this is an inquest. Real good chance his family will claim we killed ole Bruno out of malice, and staged this whole business. Or that Ella murdered him because of their failed relationship. Hell, it could go any number of ways. Not a damned one of them I can think of would be good for her."

Justin put his arm around his daughter's shoulders. "Then what do you propose we do, Moon?"

Dabbed at the cut on my head with my bandanna and said, "We could drag his sorry ass a few miles away. Dump him out in the big cold and lonely. Wolves would have him chewed up to nothing in a few days. Hell, it'll take anyone who goes out searching for him at least a week to find the corpse, if they ever did."

Seemed like a good idea to me, but Justin discarded it out of hand. "Can't let wolves eat him, Moon. Gonna have to get the law involved in this business sooner or later.

Hell, look at you. You think his disappearance and the way you look won't get connected?"

So I said, "Well, then, we'll load the body up and I'll take it to my place. Lay him out, as close as I can to the way he is right now, on my own front porch. I'll wring a chicken's neck and splatter everything in sight with blood."

Ella said, "What can we do?"

"Tidy this mess and yourselves up. Repair the damage even if it takes all night. Once I get everything situated at my place, I'll ride into town and have the marshal come out. Shouldn't be a problem convincing him that I was attacked and had to defend myself. Tales about us having words in the saloon have been flying since the day we met."

So that's the way it all shook out. We threw a tarp over ole Bruno's horse's back. Took all three of us to get him loaded. Everything went pretty good, up to a point. Arranged the body exactly the way I'd described, but ended up having to make an extra trip back to the Farnsworth place to scrounge around for Bruno's loose eyeball. Like to have never found the damned thing. Somehow, it ended up under the porch. Wasn't anything but good luck the cats or the chickens didn't get to the vile thing first.

Didn't clean myself up any. Went into town still bloodier than hell. Rousted Marshal Stamps out of his bed about daylight. He was horrified by my gory appearance. He rode out to my place, and stood around for almost an hour shaking his head. Asked a boatload of stupid questions that didn't go anywhere toward helping me explain away what confronted him. We took the corpse to town and left it with the undertaker.

Kleitz's family came in that afternoon and carried him back to their ranch for burial. Sweet Jesus, but they were one angry bunch of folks. Week later, Hector Stamps presided over the inquest. Convened the whole dance in the El Perro Blanco Cantina. Stamps figured on a sizable crowd and claimed it was the largest room in town. My

God, but he was right. Throng overflowed and spilled into the street. Didn't realize that many people lived within fifty miles of Uvalde.

Marshal impaneled a jury of what he referred to as six good men. Everything appeared to be going about the way I'd expected. That is, until the findings were announced. Turns out I'd made one hell of a big mistake. You see, when it got right down to the bottom line, small-town behind-the-scenes politics took over, and Henry Moon got a lesson in just how powerful the Kleitz clan of Uvalde really was.

Stamps accepted the jury's inquest findings from the foreman, snapped the paper between his fingers, and read, "We do hereby find the death of Bruno Kleitz to be suspicious in nature and, therefore, direct that Henry Moon be arrested and held for suitable trial at the earliest possible convenience. We furthermore direct the town marshal, Hector Stamps, to send for Judge Arthur Holmes in San Antonio to preside over such proceedings."

Well, I damned near passed out. I mean, just think about it. A whole passel of men, and at least one woman, were roasting in hell as a result of me killing them, and nothing much had ever come of those murderous acts. Now, here I was being put behind a set of iron bars for a murder I didn't commit, and in my mind at least, Bruno's death occupied the realm of a completely justifiable killing—whether I was responsible for his totally timely death or not.

Only good thing that came out the whole shooting match was I got to see Ella every day. She brought me a hot lunch and dinner without fail, and sat outside my cell door so we could talk while I ate. At first, Marshal Stamps searched everything she brought me. But after about two weeks, he got tired of that particular game and let his earlier efforts go by the board.

Damn near every day, she'd say something like, "I've talked with Pa, Moon. We'll tell Marshal Stamps the whole bloody story, exactly the way it happened."

Almost all my entreaties to her were along the lines of, "No, Ella. Don't do that. No reason to let what Bruno did to you get out. You'd never hear the end of small-town gossip. Most likely the good citizens around here would blame you for the whole tragic mess."

"Well, I worry about you, Moon."

Reached through the bars and took her hand. "You needn't trouble yourself, darlin'. I'm not trying to be noble or anything here. But hell, there ain't a jury in Texas gonna convict a man for defending himself. This farce will be over before you know it and I'll be back out at the ranch. We'll ride to Elephant Butte every morning for the sunrise. Go fishing. Sit on the porch and talk. Everything's going to turn out just dandy."

Boy howdy was I ever wrong.

19

"Gonna be fun to watch you drop."

And so, here I sat with nothing much to do but think on my sinful and bloody past. Appears ole Satan's 'bout ready to call me to book. Took almost six weeks for Marshal Stamps to finally bring Judge Arthur Holmes to town. Knew I was in trouble the moment Holmes strode into Uvalde's jail. Famed adjudicator was trailed by a cadaverous-looking gent, who got introduced around as a specially appointed prosecutor from San Antonio named Solomon Meek. Personally, I couldn't detect one damned meek trait about the man. First thing he did was stalk to my cell door and eyeball me like I was an animal with its foot stuck in a trap.

Over his shoulder, he said to Stamps, "Is this the man who slaughtered poor Mr. Kleitz, Marshal?"

Stupid jackass of a lawman didn't bother to point out I'd only been accused. Hell, no. He said, "Yessir. That's him. My God, sir, but slaughter is a damned good word. Bloodiest mess I've ever had to look on."

As Meek stomped away, he added, "Well, we'll see to

him by the end of the week." Awful part of the whole exchange was that Judge Holmes didn't say a word, only nodded his agreement.

As always, that afternoon Ella brought my dinner. Soon as she got settled I whispered, "Darlin' you've got to get me a gun. Found out this morning these people are planning on hanging me, and damned quick. I've gotta get out of here."

She threw me a perplexed look and said, "How do you know that?"

Told her all about Meek's obvious threat, and how I thought maybe Bruno's family had gone so far as to buy the judge and prosecutor. Girl said she wouldn't be a bit surprised, and promised me a weapon as soon as possible.

Next afternoon, Ella managed to sneak me a pissant-sized Hopkins and Allen .32-caliber pocket pistol. Wasn't much of a gun, but I figured it would have to do. Damned good thing she did.

Day after she delivered the gun, Stamps and a couple of newly appointed deputies dragged me over to the saloon and, quicker than a hot dry wind can lift a dead leaf, my trial started. Didn't take long for me to realize those folks intended to string me up like a ham in a smokehouse.

While not a damn thing negative about me got said by anyone from Uvalde who took the stand, I could tell it didn't matter one bit. The fix was in, and my neck had already been bought and paid for. Thank God it took a bit longer than that bunch must have figured on. Gave me and Ella a little more time to finalize a few plans. She arranged for my horse, food, clothing, money, and such, while I got ready to check out.

Stunning surprise walked into the courtroom on the third and last day of their legal lynching. The worthless drunk appointed to defend me didn't voice a word's worth of objection when the prosecutor said, "I call Texas Ranger Tiger Jim Becker." Damn, I came a hairsbreadth of falling off my chair into the floor.

Becker bumped into me as he passed, and almost

knocked me over. Took the oath and flopped into the witness chair. Meek got all the preliminaries out of the way quick as he could, and cut right to the chase.

He struck a pose straight from a gallery portrait and said, "Do you know the defendant, Ranger Becker?"

Becker needed very little by way of urging. He told the whole bloody story of how I'd killed his more-than-worthless brother in Cuero. But he didn't bother to mention Nathan's slutty wife Ruby and the ole badger game they were working.

Then, out of the clear blue, he really threw out a hell of a surprise. Said, "I've been tracking this man-killin' son of a bitch for almost three years. His name isn't really Henry Moon. I am convinced that what you have here in Uvalde is the real, live, and murderous Eli Gault—a one-man plague the likes of which Texas has never seen before." Everyone in the place that day sucked in a shocked, shuddering breath.

For the next thirty minutes, Ranger Tiger Jim Becker went through a long and detailed recitation of my killings. He didn't know about all of them, but by God, it sounded to me like he intended to get a complete list sooner or later. During his entire performance, the packed courtroom continued to gasp after every slaughter he meticulously described.

Hell, Eli Gault, alias Henry Moon, was nothing more than a dead man sitting in a chair, and two hours later, the jury confirmed it. Took that bunch of drunken yahoos less than ten minutes to reach a verdict. Judge Holmes had me sentenced to hang so fast, my head was still swimming when Stamps and his henchmen jerked me up and threw my soon-to-be-dead ass back in a cell.

One of the new deputies turned the key on me and said, "Ain't never walked a man up no gallows afore, Moon, or Gault, or whatever the hell your name be. Hear tell a man messes hisself when he hits the end of the rope." Then he sneered at me between the bars and added, "Cain't wait to see it. Gonna be fun to watch you drop."

One of his cohorts walked up and said, "Hangman's on his way from Austin right now. Marshal Stamps don't want no part of stringin' you up, so the judge sent for a man he trusts to do you up right, Moon." Son of a bitch tilted his head to one side, poked his tongue out, and made loud gagging, spitting noises. Everyone in attendance 'cept me thought him a right humorous feller.

Lawmen refused to let Ella visit me once I got sentenced. Said she could see me the day of the hanging. Didn't matter a damn one way or the other, far as I was concerned. I intended to be gone by sunup the next morning.

Waited till after midnight to make my move. The marshal and all the deputies, except for a feller named Russell Stutts, had retired earlier that evening. Stutts was the smart-mouth who told me how much fun it'd be to watch me hang and mess myself. Let him get good and asleep for about fifteen minutes, then banged on the bars with my drinking cup.

Sleepy-eyed dolt hopped out of his chair like a dagger of mercury blue lightning had struck the desk. Fumbled around for his pistol and looked sheepish. "What the hell's goin' on here, Moon?"

"Gotta go to the outhouse, Russ." None of my guards had ever denied me before, no matter how late it got. Had no reason to believe Stutts would either.

"Damn, it's after midnight. Can't it wait?"

Grabbed my stomach, bent over at the waist, and groaned real loud. Came back up, looked pitiful, and said, "Something you boys fed me this afternoon must have been bad. You can either take me outside or live with the smell for the rest of the night. Your choice."

He frowned, holstered his pistol, snatched the desk drawer open, grabbed the key ring, and said, "Damn, Moon. I'd just managed to get to sleep. Now I gotta follow you out to the shitter. Probably be up all night."

Watched as he rubbed sleep from his eyes and stumbled to the cell door. Let him get close enough before I reached through the bars, grabbed his shirtfront, and snatched him my direction. Placed Ella's tiny pistol barrel against his forehead and blew a trench all the way through his brain. Had the muzzle pressed against his skull so tight, the tiny popper barely made a noise. Dropped him quick as I could to keep the blood spurting out of his head from getting all over me.

Stupid bastard was dead before he hit the floor. I had the door open, retrieved my pistols, found my horse, and was headed for Elephant Butte in less than two minutes. Ella had told me she would wait for my arrival at the base of the butte every night till I made my getaway.

Gal was good for her word. Soon as I dismounted, she grabbed me like she was drowning, and the only person in the world who could save her was a feller named Henry Moon. Kissed me so hard, I thought the ammo in my cartridge belt would fire off. Really got my attention upon realization that I could taste the hot, salty tears on her lips.

She broke the passionate kiss, placed her head on my chest, and said, "Take me with you." I held her chin up with my finger. Light from a moon the size of a dinner plate caused her tears to sparkle like crystal. Altogether, on that terrible night of more death and parting, Ella Farnsworth was the most beautiful woman I'd ever seen.

"I can't, darlin'. In a few hours, men will set out to find me. Should they be successful, I'll spill a river of blood to keep from being taken. You could get hurt, Ella. Maybe killed. Of all the terrible acts on my head right now, I just couldn't live with that one. You do understand, don't you?"

She placed another tender kiss on my cheek, leaned away, and said, "Yes, I understand. Where will you go?"

"Been north, south, and east already. Suppose I'll go west this time. Maybe El Paso. Still pretty wild and woolly out that way. Good chance I could disappear again. Get away from all the running and killing. Sure enjoyed my stay here with you. Could've kept right on with it if ole Bruno hadn't ruined everything."

She coughed and said, "Yes, if only Bruno hadn't come back."

Put off my leave-taking for as long as I could. A final embrace, and I was on my way. Turned once to see if she'd left. Didn't seem to matter how far away I got. Ella still waved. Do hate to admit it, but of all the women I'd known in my riotous life up till then, think I actually loved Ella Farnsworth. I know for certain leavin' her that way sure hurt my heart. Don't think I ever really got over it.

Epilogue

Well, ran like a scalded-assed dog till I found Turkey Mountain. Got myself all nested up just a few minutes ago. Weapons, food, and such are all laid out for a fight. Hid the horse in an easily accessible cave not far away, just in case I have to make another hasty getaway. She's safe enough.

Pretty sure Texas Ranger Tiger Jim Becker's back behind me somewhere with a whiskey-stoked posse hot on my trail. Crazy son of a bitch has been after me so long, I doubt he'll give up the chase this time till one or the other of us is dead. Figured I'd just put up here for a spell, wait till he comes by, and kill him. Pretty sure if I put the Tiger Man down, the rest of them bastards will head back for Uvalde like scared kids.

Soon as that little task is out of the way, think I'll head on to El Paso just like I told Ella. Swear 'fore Jesus, I'm going to try my best to go straight. No more drinking, gambling, or indiscriminate killing. Do just like in Uvalde. Find me a church. Be a good boy for a spell. Hope I can

meet up with another woman like Ella. Guess I'll have to
find myself a new moniker, too. Looks like I've gone and
worn Eli Gault and Henry Moon damned near completely
out. After I shot Deputy Russ Stutts in the Uvalde jail, bet
every lawman in this part of the country knows one or the
other of me.

Well, I can see their dust off to the south. Still some
distance away, though. Maybe as much as five miles.
Gonna take those boys a bit to get here. Almost feel sorry
for them, 'cause there's not a damned one of those silly
ignoramuses ready for what's waiting on him up here in
these rocks.

Think I'll stretch out and build my self a hand-rolled
'fore this gunsmoke promenade gets started in earnest.
Might as well enjoy myself while I can. Truth is a man
just never knows how these kinds of dustups will work
themselves out once hot lead starts flying.

Just be kiss my own ass. Couple of them snaky bas-
tards must have been tracking me out ahead of the others.
Sure as hell showed up a lot quicker than I expected.
Didn't even get to finish my smoke.

Well, shit, here the sons of bitches come. Guess you'll
have to excuse me for a stretch. Gotta have to kill some
folks in a few minutes. Already have a bead on the one up
front. Damn, looks like ole Tiger Jim.